BLACK JEWEL

Bella Dama

Printed in the United States of America

First Printing, 2012

ISBN 978-0-615-66132-2

Bella Dama
PO Box 480677
Charlotte, NC 28269
www.labelladama.net

For permission requests, write to the publisher at the address listed above.

BLACK JEWEL

Foreword:

While writing this book, I kept genre in mind. I wanted one that exposed Latino people, and their culture. It had to demonstrate their spice, flavor and sensuality. I also wanted a pleasurable book with feel-good reading. And it had to deal with current, real-life issues in today's times.

In researching the available genres, there wasn't a specific one I felt my book fit into. There were a combination of many. So, I came up with Latin Contemporary Fiction.

Latin Contemporary Fiction has the following criteria:

- The main character(s) must be of Hispanic/Latin descent
- Occurring in modern or present time
- The setting seems to be or is a real place
- Real life-like stories: events in the story that can occur in real life
- Story plot includes a love relationship between people and/or objects, account(s) of human sexual relationships creating arousal for the reader and conflict or drama creating a suspenseful storyline.

As a Hispanic woman, it was important to me to have a genre that fits my passion. I hope you enjoy.

Dedication

First, I 'd like to thank my sons: Refugio, Angelo and Kristofer.
Thank you for loving me, supporting me and dealing with my
daily antics. Everything I do, I do for you. You're the reason for
my existence. I love you very much.

To my other kids: Saied, Stevie, Jossie, Schiler, Reggie, Tre,
Iliana, Hanna, Ernst and Ricky. Thank you for making a
difference in my life and keeping me motivated. I love you all
very much.

To my princess: Miliyana...I love you very much.

To Rudy and Leslie, thank you so much for your love and
support.

And a special thank you to Ms. Georgia Brown, whose name I
have to mention in its entirety. You stepped up when I needed
you the most. I appreciate you and love you.

Chapter 1
<u>The Plane Ride</u>

"Good morning ladies and gentlemen. At this time, we'd like to welcome you aboard Miami Airlines, Flight 100 from JFK to Miami International. We ask that you..." said a woman's voice making the usual flight announcements before take off.

After the safety instruction video, the flight attendants walked the aisle visually scanning between the seats of the plane. They had to make sure all baggage was properly stowed and all electronic devices were powered off.

Lola, one of the flight attendants, stopped at row 13. She saw a bag sticking out in the aisle. She asked the female passenger to properly place it under the seat in front of her. The woman turned it and pushed it back with her feet.

Lola continued down the aisle.

As she approached row 18, she saw a male passenger typing on his laptop. But he smiled, closed the top and returned the tray table to its position when he saw her coming.

Then in row 22, she saw a man on his phone. At first glance, he looked like Reggaeton artist Don Omar. But then she thought to herself, *"That's absurd"*. She laughed at herself as she politely tapped him on his shoulder. Without looking, he put his index finger up implying for her to wait.

"Sir," said Lola. "Please turn off your cell phone. We'll be taking off momentarily."

All she heard him say was "Get it done. I'll be there in three hours" and shut his phone off. When he looked up attempting to apologize, he was speechless. He couldn't believe his eyes. In front of him was this beautiful, young woman with the most beautiful set of green eyes and caramel-colored skin.

"Thank you, Sir," she said as she kept walking.

"Sorry," finally came out of his mouth as she made her way to the back of the aircraft.

Lola thought the guy sitting in 22A was really cute. She told her friend Sherry, another flight attendant on board, about her Don Omar look-a-like. Sherry had to see him for herself. So, she went up the aisle checking the cabin one last time.

"Flight attendants, prepare for take off" was announced over the intercom. Sherry closed the curtains to first class and rushed to the back to sit with Lola.

Lola was glad it wasn't a full flight. It was her last day on the job and she really didn't feel like working that hard.

Once they reached their cruising altitude, beverages and snacks were served. Sherry made sure she didn't serve 22A. She allowed Lola that pleasure.

"Hi. Can I get you something to drink?" Lola asked him staring into his hazel eyes.

"Water, please…Lola," he said looking at her badge.

She grabbed a cup, scooped ice from a bucket, poured his water and grabbed a napkin. She handed it to him with a bag of pretzels.

"Thank you," he said.

"You're welcome, Mr…" she said smiling waiting for

him to say his name.

"Hernandez, but please call me Mauricio," he said extending his hand out.

She shook his hand. "Let me know if you need anything else, Mauricio," she said winking.

He smiled and nodded.

Mauricio was the only one in his row, so that made her job easy. However, she did notice his freshly pressed suit jacket with a Dolce and Gabbana tag lying in the seat next to him. And he was wearing a Rolex. That was impressive.

After serving everyone, the ladies inched their way back down the aisle with the cart. Mauricio got a side view of Lola's butt as she slowly passed him. It was round and voluptuous. He couldn't help but stare at it as the back of her skirt pushed outwards.

Lola and Sherry stood in the back galley talking. Sherry was on the inside while Lola stood between the back area and the lavatory. In her peripheral vision, Lola saw a person get up from their seat. When she looked, she whispered "22A". Sherry leaned over to see. They looked like deer caught in headlights.

"Damn" said Lola under her breath as this tall, tanned skinned man wearing the hell out of his suit made his way to the back.

"Hi," he said.

"Hi," said Lola.

"I know I'm probably not supposed to be back here, but…" he said in a low voice. Then, he looked at Sherry, "Can I please speak to her for two minutes alone…Please?" He put hands together praying she said "yes".

"Sure," said Sherry.

She stepped out and nudged him in. Sherry closed the curtains behind her. Lola moved Mauricio to the very back where his feet wouldn't show under the curtains.

"I don't usually do this, but I can't help myself," he said.

He gently pulled her close to him and stuck in his tongue down her throat. He held her face as he passionately kissed her.

Then, he raised her skirt and picked her up. She wrapped her legs around him easily. But once things got too hot, she got down and straightened up her clothes. She couldn't believe what just happened.

She looked down at the front of his pants. There was a massive bulge protruding outwards. She grabbed it to make sure it was real.

"Nice," she said in a low voice, smiling.

"You haven't seen anythin' yet," he said smiling back.

She peeked out of the curtain to make sure the coast was clear. Then, she pushed him into the restroom so that he could fix himself. Once he came out, she motioned for him to sit in the last row. It was completely empty. And Sherry told her to go ahead and talk. The trash had been collected and there wasn't much more to do.

"I apologize if I was too forward, but I had to," he said.

"Well, I don't usually do that, but you were a pleasant surprise," she admitted.

For the next hour and a half, they continued flirting, laughing and conversing.

"Flight attendants...Prepare for arrival" was announced over the intercom. That was Lola's cue.

Before she walked away, he asked, "Can I see you again?"

"I'll be at Motions on South Beach with my friends tonight."

"Then, I'll see you there," he said kissing her hand before walking back to his seat.

Once they pulled up to the gate, everyone stood up to grab their stuff. The aircraft doors opened and passengers began exiting the plane.

Mauricio got off last. He grabbed his stuff, turned back and winked at Lola. She winked back as he exited.

Chapter 2
Lola's House

Lola was excited about Mauricio. She thought about him as she drove down the streets of Coconut Grove heading home.

When she pulled into her driveway, she saw her madrina's car.

"Madrina...Madrina...I'm home!" she yelled walking through the door.

"Míja, I'm in the kitchen," responded Ana with a twinge of a Spanish accent.

Lola ran and gave her a big hug and kiss.

Ana was Lola's godmother. She was this beautiful, exotic looking, Cuban woman with fair skin, long black hair and tight brown eyes that exuded sexiness. She stood 5'10" tall with a small physique and flawless looking skin.

Ana stood over the sink rinsing a pot of uncooked rice.

"How was your flight, Míja?" asked Ana.

"It was good. I met a guy. And he's from New York," Lola said sitting on one of the bar stools smiling like a Cheshire cat.

"Another one?" Ana asked giving her the eye.

"Yeah, but he approached me this time, Madrina."

"I know you Lola Esperanza Ana Dominguez. You're always up to no good to catch a man's attention."

"This is true, Madrina. But...he beat me to it this time," said Lola chuckling.

"Aye…Míja. What am I gonna do with you?"

Lola told Ana the story of what happened while flying the friendly skies.

"Wow. He's just as bold as you are," said Ana putting the rice on the stove to cook, then seasoning the steak.

"And he's gorgeous, Madrina. He has these hazel eyes….mmmmm. He's supposed to go to the club tonight."

"Please be careful. You can be a bit loca."

Then, a male voice said, "Stop worrying so much, Woman. She'll be fine."

"Padrino!!!" yelled Lola jumping up to hug him.

"How are you, Sweetheart?" asked David.

"I'm fine. And you?"

"I'm good."

David was Lola's godfather and Ana's husband. He stood 6'4" tall with a killer smile. This Bahamian and white man had a smooth, bronzy skin color. He wore his wavy, brown hair in a low cut and had a little gray in his beard. And he was a hunk with the most seductive eyes.

Lola told him about Mauricio. David was also surprised to hear that there was someone just as upfront as her.

"So are you seeing him again?" asked David.

"Yeah. He's supposed to go to the club tonight. So you know what that means...SHOPPING!!!" she exclaimed while prancing around.

"Well, sit and eat with us first," said Ana. "I'm cooking one of your favorites."

Ana was making arroz blanco con bistec empanizado (white rice and breaded steak, but Cuban style). And she always made it with black beans, salad and sweet plantains.

"Ok. I'm just gonna take a quick shower and get changed," Lola told Ana.

"Ok."

She grabbed her stuff and headed upstairs to her bedroom.

Lola took the bun out of her hair, kicked her shoes off and came out of her uniform. She laid across her bed thinking about Mauricio. Her fingers caressed her lips reminiscing about the kiss they shared. She was anxious to see him again.

For Lola, this was an occasion she had to look yummy for. And she knew just where to go to get her outfit. So, she called for reinforcement.

"Hey, Baby. Did you miss me?" asked Lola trying to sound sexy.

"Yes, Ho. I missed yo' stank ass," said a male voice over the phone.

"What are you doin'? Or who are you doin'?" she asked about to burst out laughing.

"I'm not doin' anything, but you know I stay ready to do somebody," said the same male voice.

"You're crazy," she said laughing.

The male voice on the phone was one of her best friends, Blair.

"Hey, I have to go to Milly's. You down to go with me?" asked Lola.

"Hell yeah! Who is he this time?" asked Blair.

"I'll tell you all about him when I see you. One hour?"

"I'll be there. Don't be late, Biatch."

"Ok, Ho."

Lola hung up and called her other best friend, Crystale.

"Hey girl," said Lola when she answered.

"Hey. You're back?"

"Yeah, but I gotta go to Milly's. You comin'?"

"Yeah. Who is he?"

"Dang! You and Blair. I'll tell you all about him when I see you. One hour?"

"Ok, but don't be late, Lola. You're ass is always late."

"Ok...Ok."

Chapter 3
<u>About Lola</u>

Lola Dominguez is an eccentric Cuban-American born in Miami. She is what Cubans would call "java" (pronounced "hava"). Java means not having white or black skin color. It is a person who is mulatto with beautiful caramel-colored skin. She is what Southerners would call a "red bone". And "javas" usually have light colored hair.

Aside from being a java with piercing green eyes, she has long and wavy, honey-colored hair, high cheekbones, full lips and a set of dimples. She stands 5'7" tall with a bad-ass body to match. She is 25 years old and an only child.

Lola is known to have many attributes. For starters, she is this feisty, Cuban girl with lots of personality, charm and sass. She is educated, smart and business savvy. She goes after what she wants with confidence. She is down to earth, outgoing and flirtatious. She loves salsa dancing, staying fit and having fun with her friends. However, she can be a little hot-tempered and she always says what's on her mind. She always stands up for what she believes in. She also doesn't care what people think about her.

Lola's major weakness is men. She loves men and they love her back. The chase and the challenge excites her. Being the center of attention is always her goal. But, Lola is a woman who mostly loves sex.

Lola lives in the oldest part of Miami, an area called

Coconut Grove. It's known for being "a village within a city". Its laid back environment mixed with upscale living makes it one of the most desirable places to live and visit.

Coconut Grove is Miami's original art district and boasts waterfront communities that are unique to the city. Its streets are filled with outdoor cafes and chic restaurants. There's great shopping that ranges from Bohemian boutiques and street vendors to high end, name brand stores. The nightlife is just as entertaining with jazz, salsa and reggae bars or the bass-pounding nightclubs. Many tycoons, artists and musicians reside in this neighborhood, which is nestled between Biscayne Bay and Highway U.S. One.

Lola lives alone in a Mediterranean styled, multi-leveled five-bedroom, seven-bathroom waterfront estate. This paradise sits on 1.8 acres of land and has just over 16,000 square feet of amenities, including banyan trees, coconut palm trees, lush gardens and a gated guard entrance. Tropical landscaped courtyards with statue water features create the perfect oasis to the entryway of the house. Etched glass designs create a luxury finish to the double front doors. The living room has a twenty-three foot high Cathedral ceiling with breathtaking views of the bay through its floor to ceiling wall of windows. Crystal chandeliers, Brazilian cherry wood flooring, custom lighting, a grand staircase, walls of French doors, four fireplaces, two wet bars and two elevators can be seen throughout the house. Her State-of-the-Art chef's kitchen has a Tuscan theme with dark, rich woods, Italian marble countertops and flooring, stainless steel appliances and a huge eat-in area. The grand master suite has coffered ceilings, Spanish arches and columns and Italian flooring. The master bath is just as luxurious. And her custom made closet takes up over 2,300 square feet of space.

Other rooms in the house include a gym; billiards room and a twelve-seat theater with a top of the line surround sound system.

The backyard has a mega bar with plenty of seating, two party size terraces, a heated infinity pool with a waterfall spa and a huge second-level, cascading edge grill area.

This one-of-a-kind grill area includes a summer kitchen with immaculate marble countertops, custom cabinetry and stainless steel appliances.

There's also a pool house with outdoor showers, a yacht, six jet skis, plush gardens and a tennis court that converts into a basketball court. Her two live-in housekeepers and chef stay in the staff quarters in one wing of the house. And her six-car garage houses her custom pink Audi TTS roadster with suicide doors and pearl white Cadillac Escalade.

Needless to say, she wasn't struggling financially.

Lola inherited her wealth from her mother's estate. Natalie, Lola's mother, passed away right after Lola graduated from high school and after she turned 18. But before Natalie died, she built an empire for herself with her baby girl as the driving force.

Natalie migrated from Cuba when she was a young girl. She always dreamt of being a model. However, just as her career began to take off, she fell in love and became pregnant. Her modeling career didn't last long after that.

So, she decided to do the next best thing: Natalie started a modeling agency. Once it grew to be one of the top agencies worldwide, she designed a lingerie line. Once that exploded, she ventured into her own cosmetics line. It also did extremely well. And she topped off her portfolio with a skin care and a perfume line with two women's fragrances.

Natalie loved femininity, so that meant fashion, beauty, scents, sexiness and romance. She was obsessed with wanting women to look and feel their very best at all times. She worked hard for over 20 years to create products that displayed her passions.

Other passions Natalie had were dancing and eating. She loved to dance and taught Lola everything she knew. And she loved great tasting food. The love for the two drove her to want a nightclub with lots of Spanish flair, great food and plenty of room for dancing.

Eventually, Natalie acquired it all. But she didn't do it alone, David and Ana were by her side the whole way.

Aside from being Lola's godparents, Ana and David are the guardians over Lola's estate. Ana was Natalie's best friend since Cuba and her trusted confidant. She was also Natalie's right hand and second in charge. So, Ana stepped in and kept the entire operation functional after Natalie's death.

David is the CFO for Natalie's entire operation. He is very smart with money. He knows which business risks to take and where to invest financially.

David made sure Natalie's dreams became a reality after she passed away. He got the nightclub up and running just the way she'd always talked about. And four more perfume fragrances were added to her already successful line.

And Natalie purchased Ana and David a four-bedroom estate a block away from her and Lola's home. She wanted them near at all times.

Growing up, Lola pretty much got whatever she wanted. Although she was spoiled, she wasn't bratty. And she wasn't one who took advantage of her mother's great fortune.

Presently, Lola receives a monthly stipend from her trust. But, she also has another source of money that she uses for her spending pleasure.

However, she wants to be like her mom. She wants to build her very own empire and add to the family fortune. She wants to explore her passions just like her mother did. Most of all, she wants to make her mother proud from heaven.

Lola loves fashion, clothes, sexiness, colors…but most of all accessories. One of her favorite things to do is to dress up an outfit with accessories. The more accessories the better and the more bling, the more fabulous.

For this reason, she started her own accessories line. She started with jewelry, watches, sunglasses, handbags, shoes and belts. She eventually wants to venture into hats, scarves and hair accessories.

Also, as a flight attendant, she saw a need for better professional attire. So with Blair's assistance, they started designing new flight attendant uniforms for U.S. Airline Carriers. She wanted to add pizzazz and style to the required attire.

Chapter 4
<u>Shopping</u>

It was a typical hot and humid afternoon in Miami. There wasn't a gray cloud in the sky and the sun was beaming.

After lunch, Lola headed to one of the best places to shop...South Beach. She went to one of her favorite stores on Washington Avenue, Milly's on the Beach. It was this vibrant and trendy boutique that carried all the latest fashions, amazing retro looks and accessory pieces to put any outfit together.

She drove her Escalade to the valet because she didn't want to hassle with finding a parking spot. An attendant ran over and opened her door. She tipped him after he helped her out.

Lola got out wearing a short, white halter dress with a floral lace design on top, pleated chiffon bottom and the same floral lace design trim on the bottom of the skirt. She wore her white Prada sunglasses and white Prada bag.

As she walked towards the front door, she saw Blair's pearly white Benz CLS 500 and Crystale's purple BMW Z4.

"Hey, Milly. How are you?" Lola asked practically screaming as she walked in making her presence known.

"Hi, Míja. I'm fine. How are you?" asked Milly walking towards her excited to see her.

"I'm great," Lola said giving her a hug and a kiss.

Lola had been coming to Milly's boutique for about four

years. Everyone knew that's where she went when she had a hot date and wanted to impress them. So sometimes, it seemed like she was there every other day.

"So, who is he this time?" asked Milly curiously.

But before Lola could get another word out, her friends dragged her to the sitting area in front of the changing rooms.

"Come, come, come and sit, sit, sit," said Blair patting the sofa cushion next to him.

"Spill it, Girl," said Crystale.

Blair Anon was her 26-year old, gay, male friend who stood 6'0" tall with the dreamiest blue eyes and jet black hair. He was Brazilian with the most beautiful tan, slender build and all the fashion diva a best friend could ever want.

Crystale Harris was her 25-year old, light-skinned Creole and Dominican female friend. She had caramel hazel eyes, pouty lips and long, dark red hair. She stood 5'7" tall with a size 6 waist and shapely figure.

Lola told them the story as she tried on clothes. She definitely told them about the kiss.

"So, that's why I have to look spectacular tonight," said Lola coming out of the changing room in a gold, mini dress with the back out.

"Next!" said Blair snapping his fingers.

"It's nice," said Crystale. "But not for tonight."

"Definitely not. Next!" Blair said again.

Lola went back into the dressing room to try on another outfit.

"So Lo…What if he doesn't show up tonight?" asked Blair.

Crystale immediately pinched him for saying that.

"It's ok, Crystale," said Lola hearing Blair's grunts. "I've thought about it. And it'll just be his lost if he doesn't."

Lola came back out in this floor length, form fitting, strapless fuchsia dress with jeweled detailing. She loved it the minute she tried it on.

"I like the dress, but it's not the right one for tonight," said Blair.

"I know, but I'm getting it anyway. I like it, too," she said looking at her backside.

She came out a few more times in different outfits and nothing was working. She wanted something scandalous, possibly red and that grabbed attention. And showing flesh was always a must.

Blair and Milly went around the entire store looking for other outfits for Lola. They came back with a hand full of pieces for her to try on.

This time when she came out, she was smiling.

"Damn girl! You almost make me wanna go straight wit all that ass," said Blair making everyone laugh.

"You look sexy as hell, Lo," said Crystale shaking her head. "I sure hope he comes."

"Me too, Girl," said Lola checking herself out. "Me, too."

Next was Crystale's turn. She had to find something to wear, too. Lola didn't want to see her in another hospital scrub or hair in a ponytail.

"You're not a med student tonight, Crissy. You're a sexy hot mama who's goin' to the club and showing off some ASSets, if you know what I mean. And I don't want to hear shit about Derrick," said Lola.

"Yeah…No conservative, doctor-to-be bullshit tonight, Biatch. It's all about the grown and sexy and being a rebel," said Blair snapping his fingers again.

Crystale knew Lola and Blair meant well. So, she entertained them and tried stuff on. Lola and Blair found her the perfect outfit.

They all got extra clothes, accessories and shoes. And Lola paid for everything. She loved spoiling her friends. They were the closest thing to a brother and sister she had.

The bill came up to almost $13,000. Lola pulled out her credit card. That's why Milly loved her so much. She always spent money when she was in there.

Chapter 5
<u>Clubbing</u>

Lola picked up Crystale in her Audi around 11:00 p.m.

"So, what did Derrick say when he saw you leaving?" asked Lola.

"He just looked at me and said your name referring to my outfit."

"Why'd he blame me?" she asked surprised.

"You really wanna go there with what you have on," said Crystale giving her a look.

Derrick was Crystale's on-again, off-again boyfriend that Lola couldn't stand. She felt Crystale deserved someone who treated her well, not used her for her money.

"Well…You look hot and sexy," Lola said reassuring Crystale.

"Thanks, Lo. So, are you ready?"

"Yep," said Lola smiling.

They pulled up to the club and her doors popped open. It was very sexy since they lifted up and not out. Two valet attendants ran over to help them out. There were screams, yells and whistles by both men and women.

Tiny, the six foot eight bouncer who Lola called her big, black teddy bear, stopped her before she went inside. He reached behind the door and pulled out a single red rose.

"This is for you," he said handing it to Lola.

"Thanks, Tiny," said Lola smiling.

"You're welcome. But it's not from me."

"Then, who?"

"Can't tell you that, but don't hurt him too bad," he said laughing and shaking his head as he opened the door.

The club was ridiculously sick. It had everything in it. Multi-colored lights flashing everywhere, escalators on each side of the club going to the second floor, canopy beds used for seating, white lounge furniture, four bars, an enormous dance floor, thumping music, people everywhere and a stage area next to the bar.

Lola and Crystale caught much attention as they made their way through the club.

Lola wore a blinged out, red jeweled bra with flared out chiffon arm sleeves, red boy shorts with layers of chiffon ruffles and red, knee high boots. The accessories she wore were from her own collection: A gold neck choker with a red rose on the side, gold chandelier earrings, lots of gold bling bracelets, a red and gold flower ring and a gold belly chain. Her hair was down and curly.

Crystale wore a blinged out, black rhinestone bra with a short, black open-back vest. Her black spandex tights were worn really low on her butt. And she had on some blinged out, low cut Red Bottom boots. Her accessories were also from Lola's collection: she wore a two-strand, diamond necklace with a large charm on the longer strand, diamond hoop earrings, lots of bling bangles, a black and diamond flower ring and a rhinestone belly chain with heart pendants on the lower back. Her hair was down and straight.

As the owner of Motions nightclub, Lola had the best seat in the house. Her VIP area was upstairs and located where she could see the entire club. And it was lit up in one of her favorite colors: pink.

"Hey," yelled Lola to Blair and Ivan who were already there.

Everyone hugged and kissed as they greeted one another.

"Damn…You biatches look fuckin' sexy as hell," said Blair.

"Thank you...Thank you."

Lola pointed to all the flowers and asked, "What's all this?"

"They were here when we got here, Boo," said Blair.

There were dozens of red roses in her VIP area.

Ten minutes later, the waitress came over and told Lola someone was waiting for her at the bar. She excused herself and walked over.

She looked around, but didn't see anyone. Then, Mauricio came up from behind and wrapped one arm around her waist, pulling her really close to him.

"Is all this for me?" he whispered in her ear.

"Well, it depends," she said flirtatiously.

"On what?"

"If you're this sexy ass man I met on my flight today," she said knowing it was him.

He handed her another red rose. She turned around and kissed him.

Mauricio wasn't suited up for the club, but he still looked good. He wore a black fitted V-neck that showed some of his tattoos with jeans and black loafers. He accessorized with yet another Rolex, a diamond bracelet, his diamond stud earrings and a long, diamond chain. There wasn't a curl out of place on top of his head. And his goatee was clean cut and well groomed.

"Sorry. Wyatt, Robert…This is Lola. Lola…Wyatt and Robert," said Mauricio introducing his friends.

"Hi, nice to meet you both," said Lola shaking their hands.

"Damn! He wasn't lying when he told us about you. You're bad as hell!" exclaimed Robert loudly.

Mauricio nudged him.

"It's nice to meet you," said Wyatt a little more subtle.

They walked over to Lola's area and introduced everyone.

Wyatt Whitfield was Mauricio's 29-year old, white male friend with dirty blonde hair, piercing blue eyes and devilish smile. He stood 6'2" tall with tanned skin and a rugged look.

Robert Taylor was his 27-year old, African American male friend with brown skin and brown eyes. He stood 5'10" tall with a muscular build, wore a low fade with a goatee and had the most succulent, full lips ever seen.

"Damn, Lo! He looks just like you said he would," said Blair.

"I'm really glad you came, Mauricio," said Crystale.

"I wouldn't have missed it," he said smiling.

Then, a Spanish song came on and Lola jumped up. She started dancing.

"Oh no…Here she goes," said Blair nudging Crystale who was sitting quite cozy with Wyatt.

Mauricio got up. "Let's go," he said putting his hand out.

"I hope you can keep up," she said confidently.

"I'll show you what I'm working with, Baby Girl," he

said confidently back.

The dance floor wasn't ready for them. They salsa danced their asses off. He spun her, dipped her, twisted her and did everything that goes with salsa dancing.

Then, a Bachata song came on. He pulled her so close that she straddled his leg. They were chest to chest dancing in tune and in sync while sliding and popping.

Finally, a Reggaeton song came on. And for a split second, everything seemed to move in slow motion.

As the lights flashed and smoke clouded the dance floor, she turned around putting her backside on his genitals. Their hands reached for the sky as her butt moved in small circular motions. Once she got into the rhythm, the thrusting and grinding got bigger and harder. She wrapped her hands around his neck, pulling him close to her. He slithered his fingers down her sides to her lower pelvic area. He squeezed her upper thighs, teasing her. She thought he was gonna go for her goodies, but he didn't.

Lola turned around and faced him. She got so close that they just kissed. He picked her up and carried her off the dance floor. Everyone upstairs was mesmerized and assumed they went to have sex from they way they departed the floor.

"Damn!" said Blair. "That was hot!"

"That damn Lola," said Crystale shaking her head laughing.

"My boy was workin' that," said Robert.

"I think I need a drink after that," joked Wyatt.

"Or a cigarette," said Crystale keeping the joke going.

Mauricio and Lola were under some stairs towards the

back of the club half dressed. They were breathing heavy and acting very animalistic. His mouth and hands were all over her breasts. Her hands were down his unbuttoned pants, stroking his penis. She wanted him to just rip her clothes off.

But he didn't. Instead, he invited her back to his place for the night and she accepted. So, they both agreed to wait since she was going home with him.

"Damn! You're alive! Y'all nasty!!" was all they heard as they drew near their friends.

"Shut up…Shut up," said Lola.

"Y'all just hatin'," added Mauricio.

They ordered another round of drinks and engaged in more shit talking.

There was an addition to the group. Janelle, Robert's girl, came out for a little while.

Janelle Blake was his beautiful and sexy, 27-year old white girlfriend and mother of his child. She stood 5'6" tall with blonde hair, blue eyes and had the cutest dimples. And she was a personal trainer, so she was in shape.

Eventually, they all ended up on the dance floor. Wyatt was really into Crystale and Lola was glad. Robert and Janelle were doin' their thang. And Blair was letting Ivan have it. Everyone was having a great time.

About 2:30 a.m., Mauricio and Lola were ready to go. Robert and Janelle had already left.

"Aight y'all…We out," said Mauricio.

"Us, too," said Blair.

However, Wyatt wasn't ready to leave yet. He wanted to hang out with Crystale a little while longer. So, he offered to take her home, but she was taking Lola's car since Lola was leaving with Mauricio. Nonetheless, Crystale agreed to stay and hang out.

Outside, a valet attendant pulled Lola's car up to the front. Lola went to her trunk and got her bag. She was prepared in case he did come.

She hugged Crystale and told her to be careful. Then, Mauricio pulled up on his motorcycle. She strapped her bag on, got on the back and put the helmet on.

"Take care of her," Lola told Wyatt.

"I will. I promise," he said.

"You take care of her," Crystale told Mauricio.

"I will. I promise," he said.

Mauricio and Wyatt dapped each other up. Then, Lola held on tight as they took off.

Chapter 6
<u>Mauricio's House</u>

They pulled into Hollywood Hills Tower. Mauricio waved his key fob in front of a square metal box. The black steel gate to the garage opened. He drove up to the fifth floor where there was designated parking for motorcycles.

In the elevator, he swiped his key card and hit '37'. The doors opened to a private foyer. He punched in a code on the keypad next to a set of double doors. It disarmed the alarm and unlocked the doors.

Lola couldn't believe her eyes. His place was immaculate. It was sleek, contemporary and decorated in lots of whites and blacks with Earth toned colors brilliantly mixed in.

He took her bag and led her to his bedroom. He set it down on the bed and began taking off his jewelry.

"You can put your stuff in one of the drawers," said Mauricio pointing to one of the nightstands next to his bed.

"Damn already!" she said jokingly.

"What?" he asked.

"I get a drawer. Do I get a key next?" she asked giggling.

"Slow down, girl."

Mauricio just didn't like a mess on his floor.

He sat at the foot of his bed and took off his shoes. She crawled up behind him and wrapped her arms around him, hugging him. He turned around and kissed her.

"So, which side am I sleeping on?" she asked.

"Sleep?" he said like none of that was gonna happen.

She laughed and then asked for a towel so she could take a shower.

He led her to his bathroom, turned on the shower and got her a towel with some feminine hygiene products he thought she might need. Mauricio always kept a small stash for his lady friends who might stop by.

Before leaving, he kissed her and smacked her on the butt.

After her shower, Lola came out in a tank top and a thong. She took a locket out of her bag before putting it away. Then, she bent over to dry her hair with the towel.

"Damn, Baby!" he said walking in the room, looking at all her goods.

"You like it?" she asked shaking her butt, teasing him.

"Hell yeah."

She popped her head up slinging her hair back. Now, she was speechless biting her bottom lip when she saw him.

Mauricio had taken a shower in his other bathroom. So, he walked in wearing just a towel, exposing his beautifully tattooed upper body. His arms and chest were chiseled and muscular. His abs were ridiculously toned and firm. And he had an 8-pack with a serious V in his pelvic area.

"DAMN, Baby! You're bad as hell," she said lustfully.

"Thank you," he said smiling, licking his lips.

She set her locket on the nightstand and climbed into bed. He handed her one of the beers he had in his hands and took off his towel. She hoped he was naked underneath it, but he wasn't. He had on boxer briefs that hugged in all the right places.

"So, what's with the necklace?" asked Mauricio sipping on his Corona.

"It was my mother's. I sleep with it for her protection when I'm away from home," she said.

"What do you mean WAS your mother's?" he asked with a look on his face.

Lola was a little apprehensive about telling him because she knew the topic could be a mood kill. But she told him anyway.

"She passed away when I was 18."

"I'm sorry to hear that. What happened?"

Lola didn't really like talking about it or getting that personal on a first date. But Mauricio made her feel comfortable. She felt relaxed and not pressured about sex. And he really seemed interested. So, she told him the story.

Her mom had been sick with what she thought was a cold or the flu. But she wasn't getting any better. And being the workaholic she was, she never went to the doctor. She thought she could cure it herself. Until one day, she was rushed to the hospital with a fever and stiff neck. The doctors thought she might have had Meningitis. But the tests came back negative. Turned out, she had inflamed lymph nodes, which caused the stiffness in her neck. And she caught pneumonia with a slight case of asthma, which explained the fever and a slight wheeze the doctor heard. They treated her with all kinds of medicine, including antibiotics. After a few days, she seemed to be getting better. Then all of a sudden, she had a heart attack and died.

"Damn! What happened?" he asked in disbelief.

The autopsy revealed that the hospital gave her a

medication that she was allergic to. It made her heart swell. And her body rejected the medicine to correct the swelling. So, she had a heart attack and died.

"Baby, I'm so sorry to hear that," he said cuddling her.

"Thank you," she said sweetly. "But that's not the worst part?"

"What do you mean?"

She told him how a certain pharmaceutical company didn't properly label one of their medicine bottles. Because one of the ingredients in that particular medication was so minuscule, they didn't think it would make a difference. So, they didn't disclose it on the bottle. And they most certainly never anticipated that that same ingredient could cause an allergic reaction that would result in death.

"Damn. I'm so sorry to hear that. How's your Pops?"

"I never met him. He died before I was born. It was just me and my mom. But she's told me stories about him."

"Well, I hope you at least sued the hell outta somebody," said Mauricio a little pissed for her.

"Yeah…Both the pharmaceutical company and the hospital. They ended up settling out of court."

"That's cool." Then he tried lightening the mood. "So, I know you got paid-d-d-d," he said in a funny voice.

"Yeah. I got a little somethin'," she said giggling from how he said it.

But she didn't like talking about the money. People's interest changed when they knew how much she got.

"Well, I don't want yo' money. I just want that ass," he said laughing.

"Can't tell," she said snapping back.

"Oh, ok. So, I see you want the dick."

"And what's wrong with that?"

"Nothing."

He climbed on top of her and kissed her. He spread her legs open and began grinding on her. Then, her phone rang. She forgot to turn it off. And by the ringtone, it was her madrina. Ana would keep calling if she didn't pick up.

Five minutes later, "Sorry" came out of Lola's mouth after she hung up.

She explained how close her and her godparents really were. She was the child they never had. So, they were very overprotective of her.

He understood.

Chapter 7
The next morning

The next morning, Lola woke up wrapped in Mauricio's arms.

"Good Morning," said Lola stretching.

"Good morning, Baby Girl."

Mauricio rolled over and out of bed. He had to pee. Lola caught a glimpse of his hardness bulging through his boxer briefs. She shook her head in disbelief 'cause she didn't get any of that. After her godmother's phone call, they wound up talking all night. But they still had a good time getting to know one another.

Then, her thoughts were interrupted by her phone ringing.

"Hello."

"Lo! Are you up?" asked a female voice.

"Crystale?" she asked concerned.

"Yes. It's me. I'm in so much trouble!"

"Why? What happened? Are you okay?" asked Lola quickly sitting up worried about her friend.

Mauricio got back in bed. He heard Lola's voice.

"Is she ok?" he whispered.

She shrugged her shoulders and put the phone between them.

"What happened, Crissy?" asked Lola.

"I just left Wyatt's house. I spent the night with him last night," she said frantically.

Crystale told Lola about their amazing night of sex and how she'd done things that she'd never experienced before. Lola laughed and told her to calm down. She needed to just go home and check out the scene. She reminded Crystale that Derrick probably wouldn't even be there.

After they hung up, Lola turned and saw Mauricio crackin' up.

"Why are you laughin'?" asked Lola.

"Dats my boy!!!" said Mauricio proudly.

"Shut up," she said playfully hitting him and laughing with him.

"Naw that's cool, though. She seems pretty straight. Better than the one he's dealing with now."

"She is. She's good people," said Lola defending her friend.

"Well, I'm sure I'll hear all about it. He's comin' over in a little bit to do some work."

While Lola got up to use the bathroom, Mauricio went to the kitchen. He went to make them some protein shakes.

They sat in the solarium and talked.

"So, when do you go back to work?" he asked.

"I don't," she said.

"What do you mean?"

"Yesterday was my last day."

"Why? Did you get fired?"

"No. It's just time I follow my dreams. And I don't feel that I have to run anymore."

"Run from what?"

When Lola's mother passed away, it was very hard on her. She couldn't handle being in Miami all the time. It was a constant reminder of who she had just lost. And she knew she didn't want to move permanently. So, she became a flight attendant. At the time, it was the only way she knew how to escape her pain. It afforded her the opportunity to travel, allowing the distance to heal her and be distracted with work.

"So, you're gonna work for yourself now?" he questioned.

"Yep. Blair and I are working on several projects."

"That's cool." Mauricio got up to put their glasses in the sink. "So, whatchu doin' today?"

"Not much. But there is something I want to ask you."

"What's up?"

"Will you be my date tonight?"

"To what?"

"Date night."

"What's that?" asked Mauricio.

Lola explained what it was, who all attends and how they dressed. He was surprised to hear how they go all out just for dinner.

He walked up to her and said, "I'd love to be your date" and kissed her on the lips.

"There's just a tiny catch though," she said scared of his response.

"What?"

"The newbie pays for everyone?"

"Ok," he said with no hesitation.

"Cool," she said relieved he didn't argue or put up a fight. "So, can you please take me home now?"

"Well, just take my truck. Then, come back for me later.

Wyatt should be here soon."

She couldn't believe the words that had just come from his mouth.

"Are you feeling ok?" she asked a little concerned.

"Yeah. Why?"

"You're letting me take the Rover? THE ROVER!"

"Yeah. Why? You don't know how to drive or somethin'?"

"It's not that. It's just after what you told me last night about how you get with your cars, I'm surprised you'd let me take it."

"Well…I think you're cool and you seem trustworthy," he said hugging her. "Besides, I know you can afford my shit if something happens to it," he said laughing.

She laughed and hit him on his arm. "That's the real reason."

Lola changed and gathered her things. Mauricio walked her down to the garage.

"Baby, put your number in my phone," he said.

"Damn, that's right! We never exchanged numbers."

"No we didn't."

"So, what name should I use?" she asked messing with him.

"What?!? Girl, don't play with me," he said scrunching his forehead.

"I was just asking."

"Where's your phone?"

She gave him her phone. He saved his number in it.

Afterwards, she scrolled through the M's looking for his name. She couldn't find him.

"What name did you put your number under?" she asked.

"Big Daddy," he said with the cheesiest smile.

She burst out laughing.

"And don't change it either," he told her.

"I won't," she said shaking her head. "But I don't know that."

"You will tonight. I promise."

He kissed her before she left.

Chapter 8
<u>*About Mauricio*</u>

Mauricio Hernandez is this beautiful Cuban and Dominican man that was born and raised in New York. His father is Cuban: born in Spain, but raised in New York. His mother is Dominican: born and raised in the Dominican Republic. She came to New York as a young adult.

Aside from his tanned complexion and hazel eyes, he stands 6'1" tall with brown hair worn in a blowout with curls on top. He is 28 years old and the oldest of two siblings. He is also a health fanatic and takes really good care of himself.

Mauricio is a confident man and sometimes a know-it-all. He also comes across as a little cocky and arrogant at times. But for the most part, he is laid back, has an outgoing personality and is always the life of a party. He is known by many and loved by all.

But there is one thing that will make him mad to every extreme...his money.

He is serious about his cash. He legally hustles for it, doesn't like sharing it and has a lot of it. He doesn't spend it frivolously and believes simple is the best way to live.

He will, however, spend money on the things he likes, for example his toys. He has a white Range Rover Sport supercharged with a sunroof, a metallic black Bentley Continental Sport Coupe and a black BMW S1000 RR superbike.

He also loves to dress and travel. In his line of work, traveling is a must. But looking good leaves more of a lasting impression.

When he graduated from high school, Mauricio left New York and went to college in Miami. There, his two loves collided: making money and partying. He started throwing parties with his friends for that dinero. In the beginning, it wasn't a real money maker. But by his senior year, he became known as the man on campus. Not only could he throw one hell of a party, but it got to a point he would rent out small clubs and spaces for events. He kept expanding and pushing himself. The more parties he did, the more in demand he became.

After college, he naturally started promoting clubs. He knew how to draw a crowd and was plugged into all the major party scenes. He grew to have a serious reputation that preceded him.

He launched his company, Clubbing Productions and became a well known club promoter, promoting the biggest and baddest clubs in New York, Miami, Los Angeles and Chicago.

He didn't just stop there. Mauricio always looked for ways to make more money. And with his entrepreneurial spirit, he built quite a nest egg for himself.

He owns a transportation service with a small fleet, consisting of two stretch limos, one luxury car and one stretch Hummer SUV. He owns two barber shops, one in the USA Flea Market on 79th Street in Liberty City and the other in 183rd Street Flea Market in Miami Gardens. He has a tow truck company with a storage lot. He has three car washes (one at each flea market and one in Aventura), a scooter rental business on the beach and fourteen vending machines in a corporate office in downtown Fort Lauderdale. And he has a healthy investment portfolio thanks to his dad.

Mauricio is venturing into opening a cell phone store, a hair and nail salon and branching into event promoting. He wants to promote any and all kinds of events, not just clubs.

But he also comes from money. Esteban, his father, is loaded.

Esteban purchased Mauricio his luxurious waterfront condo on Hollywood Beach after graduation. It sits on one of the most prestigious coasts in South Florida. His four-bedroom, six-bathroom unit is composed of 7,120 square feet of luxury living.

His home comes equipped with twelve foot tall vaulted ceilings, marble flooring, elaborate molding and impact resistant, floor-to-ceiling windows that overlook the ocean. The space includes a formal living room and dining room, family room, office, billiards room and laundry room. His grand master suite has a grand master bath, two walk-in closets, a sitting area and an oversize sunrise terrace. He uses one bedroom as his weight room, another as a guest room and the last one as his sex room. His den is turned into a game room with a 152" plasma television. But the best feature is his gourmet kitchen.

Since he loves to cook, he had his kitchen remodeled. He splurged on Italian custom cabinetry, a Sub Zero built-in, side by side refrigerator with cabinetry matching front panels and a Wolf 60" dual fuel range with double oven.

His custom-made, teardrop-shaped island doubles as a breakfast bar. And the best view is just off the kitchen in the solarium.

He has everything he needs for his active lifestyle.

In terms of women, he isn't dating anyone serious. He has female friends, but no emotional attachments to any of them. They all understand their place.

Chapter 9
The Gossip

Wyatt arrived to Mauricio's about thirty minutes after Lola left. They didn't immediately get to work. They went into Mauricio's weight room to workout a little and talk.

Wyatt went first. He told him everything about his night with Crystale and how they stayed at the club a little while longer. Then, they went to the beach. But that was cut short 'cause she had to use the bathroom. So, he offered his place since he stayed nearby.

"Where was Linda?" asked Mauricio curiously.

"Out of town."

"Ok...Finish."

While Crystale was in the restroom, Wyatt took off his shirt to look for another one. He wasn't sure where they were headed next, but he didn't want to smell like the club anymore.

She came out and saw him. Wyatt assumed she thought he was trying to make a move by taking his shirt off 'cause she attacked him after that. He didn't complain though.

"Boy, that shit was so good. She had my ass goin' crazy. It was like a monster woke up in me. I did shit with her that I hadn't done in a long time," said Wyatt excited.

They both laughed.

"Dawg, she's the first girl in a long time that's made me feel like a man and not a bank," said Wyatt.

"She seemed pretty cool. So, what's up with you guys

now?"

"I don't know. She ran outta there this mornin' after the third time."

"Damn, Dawg!! Three times?"

"Hell yeah!!! I told you that shit was good!"

They laughed as Wyatt told him a few more details. Then, date night was mentioned.

"She invited me to this date night thing tonight," said Wyatt.

"Yeah I'm going, too. Lola's coming back to get me later."

"Whatchu mean comin' back to get you?" Wyatt now asked curiously.

"She took the Rover, Dawg."

"What!!!" yelled Wyatt in total shock.

Wyatt couldn't believe what he'd just heard. He knew Mauricio either really liked her or lost his mind 'cause he never let a female take any of his cars.

"Dawg, she must have put it down last night," teased Wyatt.

"We didn't do anything, Dawg. We were about to when she got a phone call. Then, we started talking and just got wrapped up in that. We ended up falling asleep. And she even slept in my bed. My bed, Dawg!"

"What?!?" yelled Wyatt again. "No pussy and she slept in your bed? What's the world comin' to?"

They both laughed.

Mauricio told Wyatt about Lola's mother, how she quit her job to start her own business and about her godparents.

"Last night was real different for me. You know I never

let a woman sleep in my bed. And I would've fucked walking through the door. But it wasn't like that. We were jus' vibin'," said Mauricio.

"Is it possible that you, Mauricio... *"Mr. I don't get attached"*...have finally found someone you like?"

Mauricio shrugged his shoulders. "I can't explain it, Dawg. But there's just something about her."

"That's cool, though. I hope shit works out between you two."

Wyatt was still shocked they didn't have sex knowing how Mauricio was. But Mauricio assured him he would make up for it tonight and told him his plans.

Meanwhile, Lola, Crystale and Blair met up at the modeling agency. Every time they had date night, they got their hair and make-up professionally done. It wasn't like it cost them.

"Spill it," said Blair to Lola. "And don't leave out any of the dirty details."

Lola hesitated because she knew what was coming. But she told them anyway. "We didn't do anything. We just talked all night."

"WHAT?!?" they both yelled together.

"Biatch, are you CRAZY?!?! Did you see that man you were with last night? I would've raped his ass!" shouted Blair.

"Girl, I even got some and didn't plan it. Yours was planned. How did that happen?" asked Crystale.

"Well, we were about to when Madrina called me. I forgot to text her and turn off my phone," said Lola.

They just shook their heads in disbelief. That was

the dumbest move ever on Lola's part. But they did compliment Mauricio. He seemed very nice and they looked cute together.

Next went Crystale. They both couldn't believe she had sex with Wyatt…and on the first night. They just knew she was going to be the conservative one.

"When I came out of the bathroom and saw his body, I couldn't help it. He looked so good with his shirt off. It was like his body was calling me," said Crystale reminiscing.

"I think it was those drinks calling, not his body," Lola joked making everyone laugh.

"Damn, girl! So you raped him?" asked Blair.

"Hell yeah," said Crystale proud of her accomplishment.

"Look at our girl steppin' out of her shell," Blair said giving her a hug.

"Are you gonna see him again?" asked Lola.

"Yeah, I'm meeting up with him at his house for date night," said Crystale. "But…"

"But what?" asked Lola worried she did something to mess things up.

"But I ran outta his house this morning after the third time without really saying anything to him," said Crystale.

"Damn, girl! Three times?" exclaimed Blair. "That shit must have been REALLY good!"

"Why?" asked Lola.

Crystale was scared of what Wyatt thought about her after having sex on the first night. She didn't want him thinking she did that often. And she was scared 'cause she liked him. She liked the way he complimented her and made her feel like his woman all night. He would constantly ask if she was okay or needed anything. And his sex game was off the Richter scale. So, it was the first time in a long time she was excited about someone, even though they both had a situation.

Chapter 10
<u>*Date Night*</u>

It was 7:00 p.m. and Lola was on her way to get Mauricio. She was really anxious to see him. She called him while driving to his place.

"Hey, Baby," she said in a sweet tone.

"Hey, Baby Girl. Where are you?"

"I'm around the corner. I should be there in like five minutes."

"Ok. I'll be downstairs. Just pull into the valet."

"Ok. See you in a minute."

"Aight."

Mauricio saw his truck pull up and went outside. When she came from around the back of the truck, they both looked star struck. They each were dressed from head to toe.

Lola wore a red Elie Saab dress. The strapless, embroidered lace bodice had crystal beading that gathered at the waist. The ruffled skirt had a sweep train with a thigh high split on the side. It hugged her body so perfectly. She wore open toe Christian Louboutin heels and a small, matching clutch. She dressed it up with a three-strand diamond necklace, three diamond bracelets and diamond droplet earrings. Her hair was in a loose updo with some curls down in the front and back.

Mauricio wore Giorgio Armani from top to bottom. He wore a black suit with a white shirt and red tie and handkerchief. A sleek, black belt and black shoes completed his ensemble. He accessorized with a platinum Cartier watch with a diamond encrusted face, a platinum diamond bracelet and 3-carat diamond studs in each ear. His hair was freshly taped with every strand in place.

"Baby…Wow!!" said Mauricio extending his hand to her.

"Wow yourself! You look amazing," she said returning the compliment, walking up to him.

He twirled her around to see all of the dress. He stood there mesmerized by her beauty.

"Mr. Hernandez?" interrupted a valet attendant.

"Oh yes…Sorry," said Mauricio escorting Lola to the car.

There was an attendant standing on each side of his Bentley with the doors opened waiting to help them in.

"Thank you," they each said after their doors were closed. Then, Mauricio tipped them before leaving.

Mauricio had no clue where he was going. He was just driving. But the restaurant wasn't far from his place, according to Lola. It was on A1A in the Aventura/Sunny Isles area.

He pulled into a driveway surrounded by trees. Then, drove around this large water fountain with fluorescent colored lighting and stopped in front of the restaurant's valet station. An attendant opened Lola's door while another ran to Mauricio's side. He tipped them as they headed inside.

The outside of the restaurant was a two-story building with Spanish styled architecture, sconces, small gated balconies, tall bay windows, curved archways and a neon sign with the restaurant's name shining brightly.

Inside was bigger than it looked. This upscale establishment had an open layout with high ceilings, crystal chandeliers, columns and Spanish accents all throughout. There was a huge walled waterfall behind the bar as the main focal point of the room. The textured gold paneling on the walls had lighting underneath to create a romantic ambience. The seating area had high back, Italian leather booths, marble tables and contemporary and modular furniture in sunken areas. And the uniformed staff wore red and black.

"Hi Lola. How are you?" asked the hostess as they walked in.

"I'm good. Thank you," said Lola.

"Your area is ready. Please follow me."

The hostess led them to an elevator.

"You must come here a lot," murmured Mauricio in Lola's ear.

"I do," she said smiling.

When the elevator doors opened, there was a giant, plushed out room with 8' tall Bamboo silk trees, red sheer panels on the ceiling and walls, squared crystal chandeliers and an amazing view of the bay with twinkling city lights and candles lit everywhere. The dim lighting made it look more warm and romantic. And the large, Italian leather U-shaped booth with white marble tables faced the windows that overlooked the moonlit water.

"This is really nice," said Mauricio.

"I'm glad you like it."

They were smooching away when the others came in.

"Hey, Hey, Hey…Save it for later," said Blair interrupting their session.

Everyone came in and greeted one another other. And everyone looked fabulous.

Blair and Ivan wore matching suits. They wore white Michael Kors double breasted suits with pink shirts and white bow ties. Crystale wore a Dior aqua, chiffon, floor length dress with a halter top and low back. And Wyatt came dressed in a black Salvatore Ferragamo suit with a white shirt and black tie with aqua in it.

The photographer asked everyone to stand together for pictures. He captured lots of photos, including group, couples and by gender.

Lola invited everyone to sit down. The waitress came around to take drink orders while glasses of Dom P. were being served. And several waiters came out carrying trays of different hors d'oeuvres and appetizers, like shrimp cerviche cocktail, sweet potato ravioli with lemon sage butter, crab cake bites with roasted pepper-chives ailoi, blue cheese stuffed mushroom caps and Shanghai Spring rolls with sweet chili sauce. The table was filled in a matter of minutes.

As they sat around eating and drinking, Lola, Blair and Crystale explained date night in detail.

It started about four years ago. Originally, it started as a way for them to get together and catch up since they all had busy schedules. Also, it was the fastest and easiest way for each of them to meet who the others were dating and get their approval. Then dressing up and getting glamorized was incorporated when their love for fashion grew. It gave them a reason to get all dolled up. It became a rule when one of Lola's dates came dressed way too casual. Like jeans and t-shirt casual. And lastly, it was a way to enjoy great food and drinks. But they changed the formal dinner to appetizers just to keep it simple. They preferred a variety of tastes and textures to the pallet. Besides, they realized that eating a heavy dinner and then trying to have sex afterwards wasn't cute.

Then, everyone told their stories.

Lola, Blair and Crystale went to high school together. Since the ninth grade, they've been inseparable. They even got their first tattoos and belly piercings together.

Blair and Crystale went to the University of Miami straight out of high school. Crystale studied Medicine and Blair studied Design and Advertising. Blair went back to school and got his Master's Degree in Marketing.

Although Lola became a flight attendant, she did go back to school. She got her Bachelor's Degree in Business with a minor in Marketing.

Aside from their professions, they made extra money as real estate agents. Blair's parents were big names in luxury residential condos. His father was a real estate developer and his mother was an architect. Together, they designed and built high-rise condos, estate properties and commercial buildings. They were really well known in Brazil, where they lived with his older brother and younger sister.

Crystale was in her last semester of med school. She was following in her parents' footsteps by becoming a doctor.

Her father was a renowned heart surgeon and her mother was a celebrity plastic surgeon. She hadn't figured out her specialty yet.

Also, Crystale was a twin. Her sister, Carla, was married to NBA player, Bynum Douglas. He was the shooting point guard for the Miami Cyclones.

Wyatt and Mauricio met in college and became best friends. They, too, went to the University of Miami. Wyatt studied Law while Mauricio studied Business. Then, Mauricio got his Master's in Accounting. Wyatt became an attorney following in his parents' footsteps as well.

Wyatt's parents' owned a law firm with only the wealthiest and exclusive as clientele. Wyatt recently opened his own firm with elite clientele as well, Mauricio included. He had two sisters, Winter and Wonder, that loved him and spoiled him. Winter was the oldest and was married to NHL player, Mike Lassey. He played forward for the Florida Cougars. Wonder was the single, crazy one.

Mauricio mentioned that he was leaving in a few days to promote another major club in Chicago and taking Robert with him.

With regards to Robert, Mauricio and Wyatt met him at a club one night. Robert told them about his interest in club promoting. So, Mauricio hired him and they've been boys ever since.

Then, Crystale brought up Lola's birthday.

"So Lo, what are we doing for your birthday this year?" asked Crystale.

"When is her birthday?" asked Mauricio very interested.

"Oh…She didn't tell you. I'm surprised. She brags about

it all the time and will not let US forget it," said Blair with such sarcasm.

"Shut up!!!" Lola told Blair.

"It's on the Fourth of July," said Crystale.

"Thank you, Crystale," he said looking at Lola. Then said, "I guess I'll have to plan something soon, huh?"

"Are you sure you'll be around?" blurted Blair before thinking.

"You're terrible, Blair," said Ivan shaking his head.

Mauricio just smiled and said, "It's okay, Blair." Then looked at Lola and said, "But how bout we do this...You ask your girl that same question tomorrow after I've had my way with her tonight."

"Ok, Mr. Man," Blair said snapping three times.

Three hours had gone by and date night was coming to an end. Everyone was full and liquored up. The only thing left to do was get it on.

The waitress came over with the bill. Mauricio didn't even look at it. He handed her his credit card. When she came back for signature, the bill was close to $1,000. He signed and tipped $300.

Blair's black Benz SLK 55 AMG convertible pulled up first. So, he and Ivan were first to leave. Then, Wyatt's white BMW 745i pulled around. Crystale was going for round two at Wyatt's. And last to leave were Mauricio and Lola.

Chapter 11
The First Time

Mauricio and Lola stepped out of the elevator and into his foyer. He stopped her at his front door. He took his handkerchief from his suit pocket and blindfolded her.

Once inside, he guided her to his bathroom and closed the door behind him. He took the blindfold off and put his arms around her. In his most seductive voice, he said, "Baby Girl...Take a shower. Get all freshened up. And check out your gift." He pointed to a gift-wrapped box sitting on the counter. "Once you're done, knock on the door and I'll come get you. But don't come out 'cause I have a surprise for you."

"Ok," she said cheesin'. "But before you go, can you help me out of my dress...Please?"

He obliged by slowly unzipping the back of her dress watching as her backside was revealed. She allowed the dress to fall, leaving her wearing only a g-string and four inch heels. All that ass excited him. So, he slapped her on it as he left.

When he heard the shower, he finished his preparations. Then went and took a quick shower himself.

As he dried off, he heard her knock. So, he wrapped the towel around him, pressed play on the remote and went to get her.

All he could do was shake his head in amazement when he saw her. The red sheer baby doll with the matching red panties fit her perfectly.

"You called who you needed to call or text, right?" he asked making a joke, but serious.

"Yes," she said laughing.

"You ready?"

"Yes," she said feeling the flutter of butterflies in her stomach.

He pop kissed her and took her by the hand.

As they made their way down the hallway and into the foyer, there was a trail of candles along the wall. It continued into the main living space.

There were lots more candles, bouquets of white flowers and city lights twinkling through the open curtains.

"Baby, this is so beautiful," she said a bit muffled from her hands covering her mouth.

Then, she saw a huge fruit arrangement sitting on the dining room table from Edible Arrangements. The fruits were chocolate dipped, flower and star shaped and in abundance. And there were extra condiments to play with, like whip cream, chocolate syrup and cherries.

He pulled out a chair and sat down. She straddled his lap facing him.

"Do you like it?" he asked.

"Yes!!! I can't believe you did all of this for me," she said giving him a tight hug.

"I can't either," he said joking.

She let him loose and playfully shoved him.

"And thank you," she said referring to what she had on.

"You're welcome. Now are you ready for some real dessert?"

"Hell yeah."

He reached for a chocolate-covered strawberry and fed it to her. She picked a pineapple star and dipped it in chocolate. She put it in her mouth and fed it to him until their lips locked and tongues wrestled. He pulled out a stick of grapes and dipped them in the whip cream. She seductively put her mouth around it sucking most of the whip cream off. She assumed it excited him 'cause she felt his dick jump. Then, she took his finger and dipped it in the whip cream. Her tongue started at the base of his hand and slowly licked up, teasing him. Then, she put her mouth around his finger sucking the rest of it off. He watched her mouth slowly slide up and down.

He couldn't take it anymore. He jumped up and sat her on the table. He pushed everything back and laid her down in front of his chair. She scooted her butt to the edge and spread her legs open. He sat down and licked his lips at her freshly waxed and manicured vagina.

"I've waited all night to do this," he said.

With a sensual flicking of his tongue, Mauricio softly tickled her inner thighs, alternating sides. At the same time, his thumb and index finger twirled and pinched her nipples making them hard like pencil erasers. Then, he sucked hard and soft moving upwards making her body yearn for more. Her breathing became faint with the anticipation of him tasting her juices. He taunted her a little more by softly kissing and blowing on the outer edge of her vagina through her crouch-less panties. Her stomach sunk in so deep that her rib cage practically showed. She wanted to feel the warmness of his mouth and tongue inside her already. So, he gave her what she begged for.

His tongue spread her lips apart as it plunged into her already hot, juicy nectar. Her body arched up as he tasted her sweetness. He wiggled and thrust deeper into her delicacy. Her moans were loud. And her hips gyrated as if she were hula hooping.

But to demonstrate his true skills, he bent her knees all the way back 'til they touched the top of the table. He alternated sucking hard and soft on her clit until it became swollen. She pushed his face further in her cream pie. Then after a blowing, fluttering sensation, he heard those words he wanted to hear.

"I'm cumin', Baby. I'm about to cum."

He wrapped his arms tightly around her thighs and clamped down. Mauricio sucked and extracted everything she had. It made her body quiver and spasm uncontrollably.

"Mmmm…You taste so good, Baby Girl," he whispered as she pushed his head away not able to handle anymore.

He stood up and took his towel off. He pulled her back down to the edge of the table. Still high from her orgasm, he slid his manhood inside her making her back arch up again.

"Yes!" she screamed as she felt him stretching her walls with his ten and a half inches of goodness. She loved the way her feline animal was getting fed. And she contracted her muscles making it feel tighter. But that only made him dig harder, deeper and faster.

He watched as her eyes rolled back from him pounding her insides. He had his way with her.

"Fu…uck me, Baby. Fu…uck me hard…der," she barely

said.

"Whose pussy is this?" he asked as he stroked. "Whose is it?"

"Tu…yo, Papí. Es tuyo. All yours," she said.

Mauricio knew that pussy was his and he was working the hell out of it. To the point, she came again.

Lola got tired of sliding on the table from all their sweat. So, she stood up, took off the lingerie and bent forward resting her hands on the arms of the chair. She cocked one leg up extending a very open invitation to sex her doggy style. He gladly accepted.

He wrapped his hands around her waist as he slid inside her again. She just held on as he bucked her, fucked her and slapped her on the ass.

Mauricio was liquored up, so he wasn't cumin' any time soon. Lola was his toy and her body was his playground.

After she came, he pulled her up by her hair and picked her up. Her legs wrapped around his waist. He held her ass cheeks as he rocked them back and forth allowing her labia to touch the base of his dick. He wanted that kitty cat to purr.

As he delighted her g-spot, she threw her head back yelling his name. Her nails dug into his shoulders as she came again...and hard.

However, Mauricio didn't stop. He carried her to the sofa where she sat on top of him backwards. He cupped her C-sized breasts as she leaned back gripping the couch. She gyrated on him working her hole, letting him have it. His words now became slurred, sexual and vulgar.

"Whose dick is this, Papí?" she asked turning the tables.

"It's yours, Baby Girl. It's all yours."

They sexed for about another hour. Then finally in doggy style position, he was ready to release his inhibitions.

"I'm cumin', Baby. I'm cumin'," he yelled.

He pulled out and came really hard. So hard that he hunched over her for a few seconds trying to catch his breath. Good thing the sofa was there to catch him. He was weak and tired and knew he had put in work.

They lay there still, trying to control their breathing.

"Damn, Baby Girl," he said in a low tone.

"I'm sorry, Honey."

"For what?"

"For digging my nails into you."

"It's all good."

"I couldn't help it, Baby. You felt so good."

"Me? I was tryin' to rip your fuckin' insides out cause of how good you felt."

Lola couldn't help but laugh. "You're crazy," she said.

Mauricio eventually got up to get water. And Lola had to pee. Mauricio heard her fussin' and went to check on her.

"You aight?" he asked concerned.

"Yeah…I'm good."

He laughed at her as her urine trickled out.

"Well, I'm not done wit you yet," he said walkin' out smiling.

"Oh, I know."

"Jus' checkin'."

Lola sat there shaking her head, thinking *"I'm a glutton for punishment."*

When she returned to the dining room, he was sitting

at the table eating more fruit. There was a glass of water waiting for her. She sat and joined him.

"Baby…I have a question," she said.

"Yeah."

"Can I see your sex room?"

"I don't care," he said taking her by the hand.

They walked to the back bedroom. When he opened the door, she saw a bed and an armoire. Walking in a little further, she saw some type of seat contraption, a stripper pole with lights around it, a swing and some rope hanging. She didn't even want to know about the rope.

She opened the armoire and saw a stock pile of toys and items, new in the package like dildos, anal beads, vibrators, edible lotions and handcuffs. He never used the same toys on his women.

Then, she saw a collection of home made DVDs and photo albums. When she opened one of the albums, each page had a pair of panties with the girl's name and a number next to it. Not a phone number, but a number value ranging from one to ten, ten being the best. Lola just laughed as she closed the book and left.

With Mauricio right behind her, he asked, "Are you sure you're aight? You not gon' flip out later, are you?"

She motioned for him to pick her up. "That wasn't the first place I saw when I came to your house. You took me to your bedroom. So, I know you have a little more respect for me than those other girls. So, I'm good, I promise," she said caressing his face.

"Ok," he said nodding.

"Besides…I can show you better than I can tell you just

how fine I am," she said flirtatiously.

"Oh yeah…" he said smiling.

He carried her into his bedroom. She got down and pushed him on the bed. She spread his legs open and started at his inner thighs. The sucking and biting aroused him.

Then, she flipped her hair over onto his stomach as she positioned herself over his love stick. She started at the bottom and worked her tongue up. Her mouth then covered his circumcised head. She flicked her tongue on it, frolicking his hole. Then, her mouth traveled back down to the base of his cock, deep-throating it. She lubed him up as her hand stroked up and her mouth went down. She jacked him harder and faster according to the wildness of his hips. The slurping sounds intensified his arousal. He was going crazy as she devoured him.

Then, he quickly jumped up and pushed her off of him. He didn't want to cum yet. So, he threw her on the bed and got on top. He banged her like a jack rabbit, making her scream.

They were at it all night.

Chapter 12
<u>BBQ at Lola's</u>

Lola woke up in Mauricio's arms again. This time, she was sore as hell. Even he complained of soreness.

"Good morning, Baby Girl," said Mauricio.

"Good morning."

"How you feel?"

"I'm sore as hell," she said stretching.

"That's a good thing, isn't it?"

"Yeah, but damn. I haven't been like this in a long time." Mauricio just laughed.

"What's so funny," asked Lola.

"That means you've been messing with some sorry ass dudes."

"Shut up," she said giggling.

They went back and forth messing with each other. Then, she asked, "Whatcha doin' today?"

"I need to do some work, but don't feel like it," he said.

She suggested having a B-B-Q at her house. He could invite Wyatt, Robert and Janelle, if he wanted. Or anyone else for that matter. He liked the idea. So, they made some phone calls and sent out text messages.

Lola called her madrina to tell her about the BBQ. Ana agreed to organize everything. She couldn't wait to meet Mauricio.

Robert and Janelle agreed to go. However, Crystale texted back saying she was taking Derrick. Lola didn't like the sound of that. And Blair texted her, asking about the sex. She replied "10+". And she wasn't talking number value. Blair couldn't wait to hear all the dirty details.

Mauricio called Wyatt after he received a text saying he wasn't going. So, Lola took the opportunity to call Blair to find out what happened with Crystale.

When they got off the phone, they compared stories. It boiled down to Crystale was at Wyatt's house. They had just finished having sex when in walked Linda, his so-called girlfriend. Wyatt wasn't expecting her. They had gotten into a fight earlier and she told him to fuck off. Usually, she wouldn't go to his house. But, she went to surprise him and ended up with the surprise. She caused a huge ruckus and Crystale left mad. So, he didn't think it was appropriate to go to Lola's, especially with Linda. But, Mauricio still asked if he could go. Lola didn't mind 'cause Crystale was going with Derrick.

They knew it was a recipe for disaster, but they wanted their friends there.

Mauricio went to take a shower. Lola joined him. They started fooling around again. And before you know it, they were back at it in the shower. They just couldn't get enough of each other.

As they drove to Lola's, she revealed a secret to him.

"Baby, I have something to tell you," she said.

"What's up, Baby Girl?"

"The restaurant we went to last night is mine."

"What do you mean it's yours?"

"I own it. Esperanza's is my restaurant."

David purchased the restaurant for Lola on her 21st

birthday. So, date nights usually occurred there on the second floor. And the drinks and food were always on the house. She just didn't tell people about it outright so they didn't expect anything for free.

Then, she informed him that his credit card wasn't really charged. Her and her friends came up with the idea of newbies paying to see if their dates could afford it. But he passed with flying colors. Mauricio assured her that money would never be an issue.

She guided him through the streets of Coconut Grove until they pulled up to her house. Mauricio was shocked. He didn't know Lola was livin' that large.

"Madrina…Padrino…" yelled Lola as they walked through the door.

"Míja, in the kitchen!" shouted Ana.

They walked into the kitchen holding hands.

"Hi, Madrina," said Lola giving her a hug. "Madrina, this is Mauricio. Mauricio, this is my Madrina, Ana."

"It's a pleasure to meet you," said Mauricio kissing her hand.

"Likewise," Ana said blushing.

"Hey, hey, hey…I'm the only one who can do that," said David coming through the sliding glass door.

"Sorry, Sir," said Mauricio smiling.

"Padrino, cut it out. This is Mauricio. Mauricio, this is my Padrino, David."

"Nice to meet you, Sir," said Mauricio shaking his hand.

"I'm just teasing, Son. Glad to meet you," said David.

Lola and Mauricio jumped right in to help. David was outside preparing the grills. So, Mauricio offered his assistance while Lola played hostess to the guests arriving.

Blair came with Ivan and brought a bottle of tequila. Then, Robert and Janelle showed up with a bottle of vodka. Lola turned on the music as the others trickled in. Ana and David invited some of their friends as well.

David was grilling while Lola's chef prepared side dishes. There were sausages, hot dogs, hamburgers, ribs, shrimp kabobs, veggie kabobs and steak on the grills. Her chef, Julius, brought out pulled pork, white rice, black beans, corn on the cob, crab and lobster salad, fruit, chips and rolls. And Ana's friend, Susie, played bartender.

Lola and her guests were chillin' in the pool. They were drinking and enjoying the beautiful Sunday afternoon. Wyatt and Linda kept their distance from Crystale and Derrick. But Wyatt and Crystale kept playing the looking game. They'd look at each then act like they weren't.

After a while, Mauricio, Lola and Crystale got out. They went to make their plates of food and then sat on the lounge chairs by the pool. Mauricio and Lola sat on one while Crystale sat on another.

Crystale set her plate down and reached for a towel. Derrick's phone fell out. She hurried, picked it up and slid it under her towel. Just then, Mauricio got a phone call. So, he excused himself.

Crystale started looking through his phone being nosey. She saw texts from a "Larry". They read, "Sorry I had 2 leave early last nite" and "I want 2 suck it again". Crystale frowned, concerned that he might be gay. Lola could tell something was up by the look on her face. Then, Crystale read "I didn't no Krystale was ur girl. I caught her at my man's house last nite. You should keep ur chicks on a shorter leash".

She became livid 'cause that meant Larry was really Linda.

"Small fuckin' world," Crystale said angrily.

"What's up, Crissy?"

She showed Lola all the messages between Linda and Derrick. Lola couldn't believe they knew each other let alone were sleeping with each other.

Then, a text popped up from Linda. It read "I'm in the bathroom. Come now." Lola couldn't believe how bold this chick was in her house. But she wasn't going to let it slide. Lola sent a text back as if it were Derrick. Linda was to meet him in a specific room once he got into a fight with Crystale. She made it sound like he was going to pick a fight so he could storm off to be with her. Then, Crystale put his phone back.

Mauricio came back and they told him everything. They told him about the texts and the plan. He was shocked and surprised.

Finally, Derrick got out of the pool. Crystale saw Linda waiting at the bar. Linda kept looking in her direction. So, Crystale knew it was time to put on a show. And she knew just what to say to get Derrick mad.

Derrick went to get food. On his way back, Crystale started with him. After a few minutes, he did just what she wanted him to do…walk away. Not even a minute later, Linda followed. She even had the audacity to laugh at Crystale as she passed her by. But Crystale knew she would have the last laugh.

Lola carefully followed to make sure they went where they were supposed to go. Once they were inside, Lola gave the thumbs up. Crystale ran to Wyatt. She grabbed him and pulled him towards the house. Mauricio followed. Blair saw something was up and ran over to them. The others weren't far behind.

Chapter 13
The Break-Up

Lola led everyone into this closet-size room adjacent to the room Linda and Derrick were in. It had a double-sided window, like at a police station. Everyone could see in, but Linda and Derrick couldn't see out. Inside the room, it appeared as a portrait. So, they had no clue they were being watched. And it was sound proof. So, Linda and Derrick couldn't hear a word being said.

They talked about Crystale and Wyatt like dogs. They compared notes like scam artists. Linda left Derrick the night before to make up with Wyatt because she needed money. And since Wyatt was her money man, she couldn't leave him mad for too long. She was just glad she didn't have to sex him for it. Crystale had done her that favor. She hated having sex with Wyatt and did it when absolutely necessary. Derrick understood. He didn't like Crystale all that much either. He just dealt with her to make his life easier. He had several other women, but they just couldn't afford him like Crystale. Derrick also mentioned using Crystale's credit cards on these other women for hotels, dinners and gifts. Linda disclosed that she even stole money from Wyatt and told him where it was.

Her deceitfulness was turning Derrick on. So, he spread her bikini top open revealing her breasts. He sucked on them while she played in his shorts.

"Damn that's messed up," said Mauricio.

"You aight, Bruh?" Robert asked Wyatt.

"Hell no!" said Wyatt.

"Crissy…" Blair said calling her name.

"He's gonna pay for everything he did to me," said Crystale as tears of anger fell from her face.

They watched a little longer until Wyatt couldn't take it anymore. He grabbed Crystale and walked out.

"YOU FUCKIN' BITCH!!!" yelled Wyatt bursting through the door.

Linda was on her back with her feet in the air as Derrick pumped away. But they quickly jumped up when they saw Wyatt and Crystale. And there was nothing they could say 'cause they were caught dead in the act butt, booty naked.

Mauricio and Robert went after Wyatt. He was a little too close to Linda. And Lola, Blair and Ivan went after Crystale.

"Babe..." Linda tried to say, but Crystale jumped all in her face.

"BITCH, don't you dare call him Babe! He's nothing to you! He's MY man! So, get the fuck out of here! And take your TRIFLIN' ASS MAN with you!" yelled Crystale practically nose to nose with her.

"Crystale…" said Derrick trying to speak, but Wyatt jumped in his face.

"Man, I'll WHOOP YOUR ASS right now! Don't you EVER speak to her again! She's MINE! Take yo' BITCH and get the FUCK out!"

Everyone split them apart. Derrick and Linda knew they were out numbered. They were surrounded by Wyatt and Crystale's posse who were ready to kick some ass. So, they got dressed and collected their things. As they walked out, Lola threatened to call the police if they vandalized her property or any vehicles on it.

Mauricio made a few phone calls to some of his hood friends. He had a job that would pay big. All of Linda and Derrick's money, jewelry and clothes were to be taken from each of their apartments. Wyatt notified security where he lived. Crystale did the same. They restricted access and demanded the police be called if either one showed up. It was over and they were done.

An hour later, Mauricio got a text saying "done". He showed Wyatt. They just smiled. Wyatt and Crystale left to get their stuff from Mauricio's homeboys and pay them.

Mauricio stayed at Lola's house that night. Since he had an early morning flight to Chicago, he wanted to spend as much time with Lola as possible. And he wanted more sex before he left for almost a week.

Chapter 14
First Fight

It was Monday morning. Lola and Blair were excited about their newly renovated office space in the heart of Downtown Miami. They occupied the entire 34th floor of the Miami Financial Center on South Biscayne Blvd. The view of Biscayne Bay practically surrounded their 20,000 square foot space. It was prime location and near all the expressways.

"Good Morning, Honey Bunny," said Lola smiling.

"My, aren't we in a good mood," said Blair with a depressing look on his face.

"Yes! My Baby gave it to me real good last night before leaving this morning."

"Well, I'm glad one of us got some."

"What's wrong?"

"Ivan and I broke up last night."

"What! Why? What happened?"

Ivan's ex called him to hook up. But Ivan declined. He told him he was dating someone and was uninterested. But Blair felt he should have been more aggressive. He wanted Ivan to be mean and nasty. But Ivan wasn't like that. So, Blair just got really jealous. And being drunk from Lola's didn't help.

"You were wrong, Blair," said Lola.

"Whatever," said Blair throwing his hand up and walking away. He didn't want to talk about it anymore.

They worked hard all morning. They were busy getting prepared for their meeting in New York on Friday.

Then around 11:30 a.m., a courier came in with two huge floral bouquets and a Bonsai tree.

The first arrangement was full of Birds of Paradise, Asiatic Lilies and red Anthuriums. The card was addressed to Lola and said "Congratulations on all your success".

The second one was a basket full of tropical paradise, including orchids, gingers, roses, lilies and Bells of Ireland. The card was also addressed to her and said "thinking of you".

Then, she got to the tree full of beautiful pink flowers. It was for Blair. It was a Satsuki Azalea Bonsai tree with a card that read "Congratulations on all your success". Lola just smiled. It was very thoughtful of Mauricio to do that.

Lola kept looking at her watch checking the time. Mauricio should've landed in Chicago already. Then, her phone rang.

"Hey, Baby Girl," said Mauricio.

"Hi, Papí," said Lola excited to talk to him. "How was your flight?"

"It was good. I got some work done."

"That's good."

"Did you get a delivery from me?"

"Yes, thank you. I love my flowers. And Blair says thank you, too."

"Yeah…I didn't know what to get Blair. So, I figured a tree was better than flowers."

Lola laughed at him.

They talked for about fifteen more minutes. Then, he had

to go. He promised to talk to her later.

But before hanging up, he had to say it.

"Don't give my pussy away while I'm gone."

"I'm not, Baby. And you better not let no Ho touch my dick."

"I won't."

That night, they talked for like two hours. She told him all about going to New York for business on Friday. He invited her to stay the weekend with him out there so she could meet his parents. She agreed.

It was Wednesday night and it was their last night apart from one another. Lola couldn't wait to hug him and kiss him.

She lay on her bed and called him for their nightly talk. They spoke for more than two hours every night that he was gone.

"Hello," said a woman's voice like out of breath.

"Hello. Who's this? Is this Mauricio's phone?" asked Lola.

"Baby wait…" said the female voice still breathing heavy. "Yes, this is Mauricio's phone. Can I help you?"

"Who the fuck is this?" Lola yelled angrily.

"Baby…" said the female giggling. "This is Amy."

"Bitch, put Mauricio on the phone, NOW!!!"

"Mmmm…Baby you feel so good," said Amy moaning and groaning in Lola's ear. "You'll have to call back." Then, she hung up the phone.

Lola was furious. She called back several times, but there was no answer. She couldn't believe him. She knew

Amy was his ex and that he might run into her while working at the club. But, she didn't think he'd be running in her in the bedroom.

She called Blair and Crystale three-way yelling and screaming. They tried calming her down, but to no avail.

Then, like twenty minutes later, her phone rang. It was Mauricio.

"Hey, Baby," he said happy to hear her voice.

"Fuck you! I'm not your Baby! Go fuck Amy! I'm out!" she screamed mad as hell. Then hung up.

He called back several times, but she didn't pick up. Instead, she was determined to cut him as she felt she had been done.

She took two pictures using her phone: one in a short, short yellow dress with everything hanging out and the other in a short red dress that was very sexy and skin tight. She sent them to Mauricio pretending it was Blair. She asked which one she should wear on her date. Mauricio got so mad. He texted her talking shit. Then, he texted back, trying to explain. But she wasn't responding.

Mauricio was beyond pissed off and didn't know what to do. His only thoughts were getting to Lola as soon as possible.

He packed up and checked out of the hotel. Mauricio headed to the airport to try and catch any flight out. He called Robert from the road and told him what he was doing. Robert agreed to handle the rest in Chicago.

Then, Mauricio called Wyatt. He told him everything that happened. He needed his boy to look out for him. Wyatt had his back.

Wyatt called Crystale and told her what Mauricio told him. He wanted her to explain it to Lola. Crystale warned him that it would be difficult because she was hard-headed when it came to her heart. And she was convinced that something happened between Mauricio and Amy.

Lola didn't really have a date. She just wanted to go to the club and do some damage. And she dragged her friends with her.

While Lola was at the bar, Crystale told Blair what really happened with Mauricio. Blair was relieved he didn't do anything. He believed Mauricio was right for Lola. They just needed a plan to get her back home before she self-destructed.

Crystale texted Wyatt where they were. She asked him to help with Lola. He agreed, but went a little early. He wanted to peek in on them first. He was Mauricio's eyes and ears and wanted to know if there was anything to tell.

Lola was on the dance floor when some guy walked up to her. "Damn, Sweetheart!! Who are you looking this damn good for?" he asked looking at her goods in the yellow dress.

"You," said Lola smiling flirtatiously.

Crystale and Blair immediately grabbed their friend. They drug her to the bar and ordered her a double shot of Patron while they had singles. Then, they ordered another round of drinks. The plan was to get her drunk to the point she passed out. It wasn't the best plan, but it would prevent her from doing something stupid. She was hurt and looking for revenge. And this time, it showed.

Mauricio called Wyatt. He told him how he missed every

flight out and had to wait until early morning. He asked about his Baby. Wyatt told him where they were and how drunk she was. But, that Crystale and Blair were taking good care of her.

Around 2 a.m., Lola was just about passed out. Wyatt carried her out. They all went to Blair's place and stayed the night.

Chapter 15
The Explanation

Mauricio boarded his flight at 5:45 a.m. He couldn't wait to get back to Miami. He needed to explain things to Lola.

Lola woke up with a terrible headache. The room was spinning and she felt like throwing up. She'd drank entirely too much.

"How do you feel, Sunshine?" Crystale asked sarcastically, greeting her.

"Horrible," she answered.

Lola saw Wyatt and apologized to him for her behavior. Wyatt pleaded with her to hear Mauricio out before sending him packing. He didn't do what she thought he did. And he really liked her. But she didn't know what to do. She just needed to get home and change for work.

Mauricio finally touched down around 9:30 a.m. He eagerly drove to Lola's. When he got there, he rang her doorbell several times. Then, he knocked on the front door. Ana answered with David behind her.

"Hi, I'm sorry, but is Lola here?" asked Mauricio desperately.

"Not yet, Son. She's on her way. But please come in," said David.

David and Ana saw Mauricio's anxiousness. He paced the kitchen floor feverishly. They knew what happened between him and Lola. And from the looks of it, he needed to talk. So, Ana excused herself allowing David to talk to

Mauricio.

Ana slipped out the side door by the kitchen. She flagged Lola down as she pulled up. Ana told her Mauricio was inside talking to David. Lola wanted to eavesdrop. So, they snuck inside to listen.

"Can I get you anything to drink?" asked David.

"Water, please. Thank you," said Mauricio. Then, he continued, "I don't know what to do. This whole situation wasn't my fault."

"Well, do you want to talk about it?" asked David.

Mauricio didn't want Lola's people thinking the worst of him. And he respected David. So, he explained what happened.

His ex-girlfriend, Amy, went by the club he was working at. She knew he was in town because of the club owners, who were mutual acquaintances of theirs. She tried rekindling old feelings, but he rejected her. Mauricio told her he was seeing someone and wanted nothing to do with her. None of that sat well with Amy. So, she decided to try her luck another way.

She knew he stayed at the same hotel every time he was in town. So, she went to the front desk, got his room number and went to his door. She ditched the trench coat she was wearing leaving nothing, but a towel. A hotel attendant happened to be walking by. She told him she was locked out of her room. So, he opened the door for her. She went in and took $100 out of Mauricio's wallet to tip him.

When Mauricio got out the shower, she was laying in his bed naked. He immediately called security and Robert. She waited for security calling his bluff. They came and forced her out of the room. She became so erratic that they called the police. She was arrested for trespassing and disturbing the peace.

The hotel attendant told them what he did and apologized. Mauricio didn't want any action taken against him. He knew how cunning Amy could be.

However, Amy's friend who worked the front desk wasn't so lucky. She was fired for divulging guest information. She was the one that gave up Mauricio's room number and called the hotel attendant who just happened to be walking by.

Amy thought she could lure Mauricio into having sex with her, but not this time. Mauricio even showed David the incident report from the hotel to corroborate his story.

Next, Mauricio told him what Amy did when Lola called. To piss her off and make her jealous, she pretended they were fooling around. But he was never there. Lola never heard his voice. And he could only imagine how convincing Amy sounded. But Lola wouldn't talk to him so that he could explain.

David was amazed at what Mauricio went through. He advised him to fight for Lola. He knew his goddaughter. She liked him. She was just hurt by what happened. In her mind, he betrayed her. But Mauricio assured him he hadn't.

David offered Mauricio some advice. He welcomed it.

The first thing David told him to do was to plead and leave. Mauricio didn't understand what that meant. So, David explained.

When a woman's truly fed up, nothing will change her mind. Men try to apologize with gifts and flowers. But that won't bring her back. So, Mauricio just needed to plead his case and leave it alone. Ultimately, it was the woman's choice to be with him or not. And only if she forgave him should he shower her with gifts and flowers. That way, he doesn't spend money in vain. Mauricio agreed.

The second thing he told him was to take preventative measures when he really cared about a woman. Mauricio shouldn't have put himself in that position, especially if he knew how Amy was. David wasn't blaming him. He was just trying to point out where some of the responsibility lay. David knew Mauricio couldn't control Amy's actions. But he could control his. And at the end of the day, it didn't matter whose fault it was or who was to blame. Mauricio had to fix it. And by taking preventative measures, he could have avoided most of what happened. For example, change hotels if she knew where he was staying. Or hire a security guard. Something. Anything. He just needed to do something extra to protect himself. It would be easier going the extra mile than trying to repair a damaged woman's heart. Mauricio agreed again.

He understood everything David told him and appreciated the talk. He just needed Lola to come so he could fix things.

"Hi, Padrino," said Lola interrupting them.

"Hi, Míja," he said.

David hugged Lola and told her to go easy on him. Then, he shook Mauricio's hand and wished him well. Mauricio thanked him for everything.

Lola and Mauricio were left alone. He immediately apologized and told her the same story he just told David.

He even showed her the incident report. She listened and allowed him to explain himself even though she overheard everything.

Her padrino always taught her to let a man say what he needed to say. Allow him to speak and tell his side of any story, even if she did know the truth. 'Cause if she didn't, she may not get an explanation when she really wanted one.

Lola forgave him. He hugged her really tight.

"I'm sorry, Baby. I never meant to hurt you," he said wiping a tear that rolled down her face.

"I'm sorry, too. But hearing her say those things was hard."

"I know. She can be very convincing."

"You wanna know what it boils down to Mauricio?"

"What?"

"A woman doesn't want to share the person that makes her feel amazing. Or alive and happy. And you do that. You make me feel that way. And I know we've only known each other a very short time, but there's just something about us that I can't explain. We have this strong connection. I feel safe and secure with you. I feel comfortable with you. So, when she picked up your phone, my heart just fell to the floor."

"Baby, I understand. And I'll be honest with you. The women I meet never seem to have what I'm looking for. They just serve a purpose. But you…You're smart, funny and beautiful. And I can't explain it either, but I find myself thinking about you all the time. I don't want anyone else touching you. And I don't want to share you. I can't lose you, Lola."

She caressed his face before they kissed. He picked her up and carried her to the bedroom.

They lay on her bed making out. Then, Lola stopped Mauricio.

"If you ever want to be with someone else, let me know and…" Lola started to say, but he wouldn't let her finish. He covered her lips with his finger.

He silently looked at her and into her eyes, gently caressing her face. "I don't want anyone else, but you. I can't even think about not being with you." Then, he said those words a girl always wants to hear.

"I think I love you."

She laughed at him and said, "I think I love you, too."

They made sweet and passionate love all morning.

By late afternoon, Lola was on the phone with Blair making sure everything was ready for tomorrow's meeting. Once everything was set, they headed to the airport to catch their plane to New York.

Chapter 16
<u>Meeting in New York</u>

It was 7:40 a.m. Friday morning. Lola and Blair were super excited. They stood outside on Lexington Avenue at the entrance of the Chrysler Building. They looked up. Then, they looked at each other.

"This is it, Blair," said Lola.

"This is what we've worked so hard for, Lo," said Blair.

They walked through the triangular shaped lobby admiring the Art Deco glam, which included red Moroccan marble walls, sienna-colored flooring, sconces, chandeliers and the exuberant rare wood marquetry on the elevator doors. But, the best part was the famous ceiling mural. Eyes couldn't help but gaze upwards at the intricate details of it. It was over the top and drew the most attention.

A black-haired woman met them as they exited on the fiftieth floor. She led them to one of the meeting rooms so they could set up for their presentation.

With the airline executives in attendance, Lola and Blair began the meeting.

First, they presented their designs for the new flight attendant's uniforms. Blair demonstrated the different colors, fit, style and fabrics used to create them. The bright, but bold colors grabbed their attention immediately. They appeared stylishly upscale and made of quality. And they loved the personalization for each airline.

Models were brought in to exemplify the actually look

and fit. Lola saw heads nodding up and down expressing their approval.

Next, Lola and Blair discussed cost and distribution methods. It was about giving the airline professionals style while still being competitive. So, they made sure to offer these new uniforms at competitive pricing. Lola and Blair also discussed vendor options to accommodate the airlines as desired.

And last, Lola told her story of being a flight attendant. She explained why she felt changes were imperative. They agreed with some of her points.

Everyone shook hands after the meeting. Lola and Blair came out feeling confident. But, they still had to wait for the official word.

As they were leaving, Blair saw an old friend. He excused himself momentarily to say hello. Lola continued walking out. She waited for him in the car.

Back at the hotel, Mauricio couldn't wait to hear all about it. They walked in ranting and raving about how well the meeting went. They both started explaining, trying to out talk the other. But then, they did this whole tag team routine. Blair would talk, then Lola would finish. Or Lola would talk, then Blair would finish. Mauricio couldn't help but laugh at them.

When they were done, he complimented them. He spoke on their talent and felt they had nothing to worry about. They had it in the bag.

Mauricio invited Blair to have dinner with them and his parents. Blair thanked him, but he had plans. He was going to hang out with his friend, Ricky, who he had just run into.

They used to hook up when Ricky lived in Miami. Now, he was in New York and they were going to "catch up" according to Blair. Lola knew what that meant. She told him to call and check in with her later. Blair laughed and said not if he was lucky. Then, he bid Lola luck regarding the parents and left.

Chapter 17
Mauricio's Parents

Mauricio's parents stayed near the hotel. So, their ride down Park Avenue was short. They pulled in front of this elegant limestone clad building and got out. The doorman immediately recognized Mauricio and let them in.

In the elevator, Mauricio asked Lola not to talk about her money in front of his mom. She would see why. Lola agreed.

When they got off on the sixteenth floor, his father, Esteban, was standing in the private foyer waiting for them. He hugged Mauricio tight. Then, Mauricio introduced him to Lola. Esteban hugged her too. Maritza, his mother, greeted them as well and invited them in.

Esteban Hernandez stood 6'2" tall with blue eyes and short salt and pepper hair. He had that caramel, honey skin color, muscular build and a beautiful smile. Lola found him to be very attractive for an older man.

Maritza Hernandez was 5'7" tall with bronzy skin, brown eyes and brown hair. She was thin and kept in shape. She wore a really cute, but short haircut with long bangs.

But Maritza was one of those types of women that kept up with the Joneses. She used every beauty product on the market to stay looking young. She had to have all of the latest. And she was a celebrity groupie. Any event she heard about that a celebrity might be at, she was there.

"So, where are you guys staying?" Esteban asked

Mauricio with a slight Spanish accent.

"At the Grand Hyatt down the street."

"You know you could've stayed here."

Maritza just gave Esteban a look. Lola saw it.

"Don't worry, Dad," said Mauricio.

As they engaged in conversation, Lola paid close attention to Maritza. She could tell Maritza wasn't too fond of her. She made noises or slick comments after Lola's answers to questions asked. Lola was shocked and a little saddened by Maritza's behavior. This was Mauricio's mother and she wasn't giving Lola a fair chance. However, Lola wasn't the type to let anyone disrespect her either. And she sure as hell wasn't going to start now. But, she kept her cool for Mauricio's sake.

"So, Lola…What do you do for a living?" Maritza asked with a thick New York accent. "Or are you employed?"

Lola just laughed. This woman couldn't be for real.

"Here we go," said Mauricio under his breath.

"Yes I work. I'm a flight attendant for Miami Airlines," said Lola heeding Mauricio's advice.

"Oh I see. So what working class is that?"

"Excuse me…" said Lola fed up.

"Ma…Cut it out. I know what you're doing," Mauricio told her.

"Maritza…Enough. Don't be rude," said Esteban in a stern voice.

Esteban explained that Maritza had someone in mind for Mauricio. It was a friend's daughter named Tathlia. But Mauricio never found an interest in her. The problem was Maritza didn't seem to understand that. She consistently pushed her on him. It was because Tathlia's family was wealthy. Maritza was all about the money. And the one with the most was whom she wanted in the family.

Lola finally understood why Mauricio said what he did in the elevator.

Maritza excused herself to make a phone call. Esteban and Mauricio knew she was up to something. But since they didn't know what yet, they dismissed it.

In her absence, Esteban apologized for his wife's behavior. She meant well, but it was difficult to see sometimes.

Mauricio told Lola it was safe to talk around his dad. So, Mauricio told Esteban why she was really in New York and about her house, chef and yacht. Lola didn't need his money like Maritza had been insinuating.

"She's the one, Papí," said Mauricio pulling Lola close to him.

"I'm happy for you, Míjo," said Esteban.

Maritza came back smiling. She planned a luncheon for them on Saturday afternoon. She invited family and friends over. Mauricio and Esteban knew what that meant. But Mauricio and Lola agreed to attend anyway.

Then, Mauricio's brother, EJ (Esteban Jr.) walked through the door.

"Hey, Bruh!!!" yelled EJ. He hugged Mauricio and then saw Lola. "Damn! Who's this?" he asked trying to push Mauricio out of the way.

"Slow down, Bruh," Mauricio said blocking him. "This is my girl, Lola."

"Hi," said Lola smiling and waving.

EJ pushed Mauricio out of his way and gave her a hug.

"Hey girl," said EJ. "You're fine as hell. You got any sisters?"

"Thank you and no," she said laughing.

EJ was also very handsome. He was 24 years old with a rambunctious personality, very outspoken and very honest. He looked like a mini Esteban with black hair, but had green eyes. He stood 6'0" tall with long braids. He was definitely a pretty boy.

"Ok…Everyone's here. Let's go," said Esteban.

Esteban invited the kids to eat sushi. A friend of his opened a new restaurant down the street. So, he took his family to its opening night.

Lola and Mauricio went in their car. Esteban and Maritza rode in his smoke gray Bentley Continental GT. And EJ drove his white and black Ferrari 599 GTB Fiorano.

They walked into the restaurant and was immediately greeted by the owner. He had Esteban and his family seated right away.

After the waiter took their orders, Maritza started again."So, Lola…Have you ever eaten sushi before?"

"Are you serious?" asked Lola in disbelief. "My chef makes it for me all the time."

Mauricio nudged her.

"Chef? On a flight attendant's salary? Yeah, right," said Maritza making herself laugh.

"Maritza! Enough!" said Esteban getting angry.

"Don't tell me Ma is showing out cause of Tathlia?" asked EJ.

"Yeah, man. She's on it," said Mauricio.

"Lola, don't pay her any attention. She does this to scare off any girl Mauricio likes. Unless of course, you have lots of money. Or you're Tathlia," said EJ.

"Esteban Jr.!" exclaimed Esteban in a low voice.

"Papí, it's true. You know she's money hungry," said EJ.

"Enough! From you and your mother. Enough!" Esteban said very disappointed. "Lola, I apologize for my family's behavior."

"It's ok. You and EJ have been great," she said making a point to exclude Maritza.

They survived the rest of dinner without any more insults from Maritza. EJ even held his tongue.

EJ loved to party. He made it his business to know the happenings of New York. So after dinner, he invited Mauricio and Lola to go clubbing. They agreed to go, but had to change first. So, everyone said their good byes and went their separate ways.

Chapter 18
<u>The Luncheon</u>

The next morning, Blair and Ricky stopped by Lola and Mauricio's suite to hear all about their evening. Blair couldn't believe Maritza's behavior towards Lola. And it was even more surprising Lola didn't go off.

Mauricio told them about the infamous luncheon at his parents' house. Blair would definitely be in attendance this time. After all he heard about Maritza, he didn't want to miss the show.

They arrived to his parent's house around two in the afternoon. There were several guests already there. And Maritza had a spread of appetizers out for people to munch on.

Esteban was talking to Lola and her friends when his twin sisters, Carmela and Camelia, showed up. They were almost identical, except Carmela had green eyes while Camelia had brown ones.

Mauricio introduced everyone to his family. Camelia complimented Mauricio on how beautiful Lola was. Several comments were made about Lola resembling Carmela. Maritza, of course, made faces.

After about twenty minutes, Tathlia walked in. Maritza was full of smiles then.

"She's startin' man," said EJ to Mauricio. "Watch yo' back."

"I know…I see her," said Mauricio agitated.

Maritza went around the room introducing Tathlia. When she got to Lola and Mauricio, she introduced Lola as Mauricio's friend. He quickly corrected her and advised her to stop with the games or he'd leave. Then, took Lola's hand and walked away.

Esteban went over by the window where they were talking. He apologized to Lola yet again. Maritza's behavior was embarrassing and he didn't want her to feel awkward. Lola told him to stop apologizing for her. It wasn't his fault. She was a grown woman in control of her own actions. And she knew exactly what she was doing. But Lola warned him that she wasn't gonna take much more of her crap. She was trying to be respectful because she was Mauricio's mother. But she didn't allow anyone to treat her that way.

He understood.

Mauricio stepped away to talk to his dad and brother. Tathlia saw Lola and her friends talking to Camelia and her husband, Wayne. So, she felt it was the perfect opportunity to try and ruffle Lola's feathers.

She walked over, but only got looks.

"What do you want, Tathlia?" asked Camelia.

"Just wanted to come and talk with you guys. I wanted to get to know Mauricio's friend a little bit better," she said trying to start some mess.

Lola laughed.

"Just leave," said Camelia.

"And Bitch, I'm not his friend. I'm what you will never be," added Lola with a smile.

"Such language. You didn't have to call me that," Tathlia

said sounding proper and preppy.

When Esteban saw who was by Lola, he showed Mauricio.

Mauricio walked over with such fury. His mother had gone too far this time.

"Let's go," he said grabbing Lola's hand. Then, he called Blair and Ricky to leave as well.

He gave his aunts a hug and kiss. Lola, Blair and Ricky followed suit. Everyone said their good-byes.

But since Mauricio was leaving, so was Esteban's side of the family. They were only there because of him. They couldn't stand Maritza.

As Mauricio and his guests approached the door to leave, Tathlia tried to touch him. Lola grabbed her hand and pushed her aside. "Bitch, step off," she said walking out.

Maritza tried to defend Tathlia.

"Lola, don't talk to her like…" Maritza started to say, but Lola jumped in and blurted, "Shut the fuck up!!" to his mom. Maritza couldn't believe Lola had just done that.

In the lobby, everyone gave Lola accolades. Carmela and Camelia loved how she defended Mauricio and stood up to Maritza and Tathlia. They were tired of seeing Maritza push that girl on their nephew. Esteban loved her feistiness. EJ just hugged her.

Then, Lola apologized to everyone, especially Mauricio. She didn't want to be nasty, but her buttons were pushed. Everyone told her not to worry about it. And Mauricio totally understood why she did what she did.

He actually apologized to her. He didn't know his mother would be that unbearable. But, he really wanted her to meet his dad.

Since they had no plans, Mauricio suggested they spend the rest of the day at Coney Island. He hadn't been there in years and thought it would be a good distraction. Everyone went, including Esteban.

They rode the rides, ate Nathan's hot dogs, played games and won prizes. Everyone got along so well and had a great time.

Then, Esteban led Mauricio and Lola down the Boardwalk. He told them about a fond memory that happened there.

He proposed to his true love, Amelia, right where they stood. He expressed much admiration for her. She was the most beautiful woman in the world. And her eyes made anyone's heart melt. He wanted to spend the rest of his life with her. They were supposed to get married.

"Why didn't you?" asked Lola.

The day Amelia and him were supposed to get married, he didn't show up for the wedding. The reason was because Mauricio got sick and ended up in the hospital. But Amelia assumed he wanted to be with Mauricio's mother, Maritza, as oppose to her. However, that wasn't the case.

As soon as he could, he flew to where Amelia was to explain what happened. Unfortunately, he wasn't able to. Instead, he got into an altercation with her outside of a restaurant because she was with another man. Later that night, he went to apologize and try again. But from the looks of things, he was too late.

Chapter 19
Lola's Birthday Meeting

They returned from New York in the early afternoon on Sunday. Lola called a meeting to discuss her birthday plans. She asked everyone to meet at her house. She even invited Robert and Janelle to partake in her birthday celebration.

Everyone arrived by 6:00 p.m. Her chef prepared some delicious snacks and cocktails while they waited for dinner.

Lola jumped right in with suggestions for travel destinations.

"What if we go to Europe?" suggested Lola.

"What about Vegas?" suggested Robert.

"What about the Grand Canyon or a camping trip?" suggested Wyatt since he was an outdoorsy person who loved dirt biking, fishing, hiking.

"Sorry, Wyatt…But hell no!" said Lola laughing.

"What about a cruise somewhere?" suggested Mauricio.

Lola saw that the newcomers didn't quite understand what she meant by vacation. So, she broke it down.

Her birthday celebration usually started on a Wednesday and ended on a Sunday. The goal was to try a new destination spot each year and have one special thing each day. They usually departed early in the morning so they could enjoy as much of the first day as possible. They stayed at the best hotels, ate the finest cuisines and partied like rock stars. Their activities would include eating, drinking, shopping, clubbing, sexing and whatever else they felt like doing. Transportation was provided. And sleep deprivation was a possibility. All everyone had to do was show up. She paid for the whole thing.

So, they got serious about their suggestions. Eventually, everyone decided on island hopping. They thought it would be fun visiting a different island each day. Aruba, Turks and Caicos, the Cayman Islands and Cancun were the islands of choice. And although Cancun wasn't really an island, it was still a great place to party.

"Baby," said Mauricio.

"Yeah," Lola responded.

"Why don't we end your birthday celebration in New York?" asked Mauricio. "I was planning something special that Saturday and I'd like for my family to be there, too."

"And that actually sounds good to me," said Blair. "I'm taking Ricky and he has to be back in New York by Saturday afternoon. So that's perfect."

"Okay. We'll spend my birthday in New York," said Lola. "But that means we have to give up an island."

Everyone agreed the Cayman Islands were out.

So with the destinations out of the way, Lola could go over the rules.

First, they needed passports. Second, they couldn't take suitcases. Nothing! Third, they had to wear their bathing suits under their clothes they were traveling in. Fourth, they had to be willing to try new things. Fifth, they MUST drink. And last, everyone had to stay at Lola's on that Tuesday night before the trip. That way, everyone could leave together early Wednesday morning.

No one had a problem with the rules. But they really had

no idea what they were getting ready to encounter. She told them to expect great surprises.

"Are you sure about footing the bill for all of us?" asked Robert.

"And what are we gonna wear?" asked Janelle.

"Yes. I'm positive. I'll take care of everything, Robert" said Lola. "And that's what shopping is for, Girl."

"Don't worry about it. She's got money," said Blair.

"Yeah, but that doesn't mean she wants to spend it on us," said Robert.

"Robert, trust me. Just show up with your swimming trunks on and be ready to party," assured Lola.

Mauricio couldn't believe her generosity. But, she did that so no one had to worry about spending what they didn't have. For her, the sky's the limit. So, she did it big on birthdays. And ultimately, she just wanted everyone to have a great time.

Then, Lola asked them to give David some personal information in order to make the necessary travel arrangements. He also took their picture for a surprise Lola had for them.

Mauricio jumped in and offered to provide the transportation to the airport. It was the least he could do.

Dinner was done. So, everyone adjourned to the dining room to eat. There was much excitement flowing through the room.

David and Ana announced they weren't going island hopping with them because they had other plans. But they would definitely be in New York on Saturday.

Mauricio pulled her godparents and two best friends

aside. He wanted to discuss some of his surprises he had for her birthday. They all loved what he had in mind. Blair told him to include the Plaza Hotel. It was one of her favorites. They all gave input on how things should look. And David and Ana were adamant about paying for it.

Chapter 20
<u>*Wednesday: Cancun*</u>

It was finally time for Lola's birthday celebration.

Mauricio received a phone call from the limo driver early Wednesday morning. He was outside and ready to take them to the airport.

Before walking out the door, Lola grabbed her Coach duffle bag. It had all essential paperwork and items inside necessary for the trip.

As their Hummer limo drove up to General Aviation, they saw flashing lights. Lola hired a videographer and photographer to capture their departure. The limo stopped at a red carpet in front of a private jet.

"Damn! Now this is what I'm talking about!" said Robert overjoyed.

They got out coupled for the pictures. Then, several group pictures were taken by the limo and on the stairs of the jet.

Lola rented a Gulfstream V. This 15-passenger jet had a lavish interior, including white leather seating with black cherry wood furnishings, plush carpeting, swivel chairs, a sofa, plasma TVs and a fully stocked mini-bar. And there was ample room for them to move around.

The flight attendant handed each passenger a glass of champagne as they took their seats. Everyone toasted to a fabulous island hopping birthday celebration.

Lola reached in her bag and pulled out brand new digital

cameras and camcorders for everyone. She asked that lots of pictures and videos be taken throughout the trip. She was creating an album for her birthday and wanted as many memories as possible. Everyone gladly obliged.

With everyone strapped in, they were cleared for take off. Their first stop…Cancun, Mexico.

Two and a half hours later, the pilot announced, "Welcome to Cancun. The time right now is 9:56 a.m. The high will be 81 degrees today and plenty of sun. Please enjoy your stay."

Everyone looked out of the windows and saw four white Cadillac Escalades parked. Lola politely asked the flight attendant to film them coming out of the plane. Lola tipped her big for the favor.

When the aircraft doors opened, the first Escalade pulled up to the red carpet. Wyatt and Crystale got off first. Robert and Janelle got in the second Escalade that pulled up. Blair and Ricky got in the third one. And Lola and Mauricio went last.

As they caravanned up to the hotel, palm trees lined the streets. From a distance, they saw five golden, mountainous pyramids with the tallest one in the middle. It reminded them of Egypt and ancient Mayan ruins.

They pulled around to the backside of the middle building. This was the VIP entrance into the hotel. They were escorted to an exclusive lounge area for private check-in. Four women with tablets in their hands walked over.

"Good morning. Welcome to the Grand Melia Cancun Hotel and Resort. My name is April and I will be one of your personal assistants today," said this red-haired woman greeting them.

A waiter came over with glasses of champagne for everyone.

"This is Raquel, Silvia and Luz," said April assigning each couple their very own personal assistant.

Each couple sat with their lady to finish the check-in process. Afterwards, Lola asked to speak to the assistants privately.

They went into a room and closed the door. Lola pulled out seven named gift bags from her duffle bag. She asked that each one be placed in their couple's room and gave instructions.

Once they came out, April and the other ladies went to the front desk to pick up envelopes.

"Okay. Please follow us," said April.

Everyone got up and followed their assistant.

"Hey! Meet back down in a half hour by the pool," yelled Lola.

"Ok…Aight…Ok..." was all she heard as they walked off in different directions.

April was Lola and Mauricio's assistant. She told them about the hotel's services and amenities as they entered their private elevator. And as they rode to the top floor, she went over special privileges offered by the hotel that they were entitled to because of where they were staying.

"Welcome to the Presidential Suite," said April opening the doors.

While April did what Lola requested, Lola and Mauricio embraced the beauty of this 4,000 square foot space. The beiges and tans complimented the dark wood flooring. And the shades of oranges, reds and yellows added liveliness to this contemporary styled suite.

"You have two whirlpools, a rain shower and a private terrace. You also have your own butler, maid service and nightly turndown service," said April as she approached them.

She went over other features of the room and answered their questions.

"Ok…Well here are your room keys and your $100 bar cards," said April handing Mauricio the envelope. "Here is my card in case you need anything. Please review your welcome packet on the table. And I will see you in a little while. Enjoy your stay."

Mauricio grabbed Lola and kissed her. "Baby, this is really nice. Thank you."

"You're welcome. Now come. I have a surprise for you," she said pulling him towards the master bedroom.

On the bed, sat a gold gift bag with his name on it.

"What's this?" asked Mauricio.

"Open it."

Mauricio opened the bag and pulled out a black box. The note on the outside said, "Shop 'til you drop. Love you." When he opened it, he saw a credit card with his name and picture on it, cash and a pouch.

He counted the cash and there was $5,000. He couldn't imagine what was on the card.

"Baby, what's all of this?" he asked.

She gave each person $25,000: $5,000 in cash and $20,000 on the credit card. That's why she didn't want them to bring suitcases. Everyone would shop like her and spend like her without worrying about cost.

The credit card was to be used at the mall. The cash was in case they wanted to buy souvenirs from street vendors. And the pouch was to hold their personal items, like the room key, credit cards, money, ID, etc. It went around the neck, so it was easy to carry. And it was waterproof, so they could have it by the pool.

It was unheard of what she had done.

"Baby, I want my pussy right now," Mauricio said falling more in love with her.

She took off his shirt as he took off her dress. His shorts fell to the floor as she lay on the bed. She slid her bikini bottoms off and spread her legs open. He gently swiped his finger between her sweetness and tasted her. Then, he slid his hard erection inside of her. Her hips gyrated as he pushed deeper inside. Their moans got louder. They were like two mating animals indulging in a mid-morning quickie.

Everyone was already downstairs when they eventually made it.

"Hey," said Lola cheesin' from ear to ear.

"Y'all nasty," said Crystale laughing, knowing why they took so long.

"So," said Lola laughing too.

The waiter approached Mauricio and Lola as they sat on their lounge bed by the pool.

"Hi. My name is Miguel and I'll be your server. What can I get for you today?"

They ordered four mango Mojitos. And that was just for them. She also asked for a food menu. Everyone was hungry and needed something to soak up all the alcohol.

Robert and Janelle walked over and immediately thanked her. Wyatt and Ricky were right behind them. Everyone was so appreciative of what she had done with regards to the Presidential Suite, money and credit card.

Miguel came back with their drinks and gave them a few minutes to look over the menu. When he came back, they ordered two of each: shrimp cocktail, coconut shrimp, fried taco roll-ups, fruit, crab cakes, fried cheese, quesadillas with chicken and steak and chips with salsa. And Blair ordered another round of drinks with shots of Patron.

For the next couple of hours, they played games in the pool, laid out in the sun, ran up their bar tab and just had a blast.

Then, April and the other ladies came over with two towels and two robes in their hands for each of their couples. It was time for them to move on to their next planned activity. So, everyone dried off and put their robes on.

They paid their bar tab with six of the eight $100 bar cards received by the hotel. And each one tipped Miguel with a hundred dollar bill.

April led them through the VIP lobby and out the front door. There, two of the four Escalades were waiting. Everyone wanted to know where they were going, dressed the way they were. But it was a surprise. This was Lola's special thing for the day.

They pulled up to a nearby hotel. They saw two hotel attendants standing outside. As they got out, the gentlemen introduced themselves.

"Hi. My name is Jose and this is Ortiz. Welcome to Dreams Cancun Hotel. Please follow us."

They walked through the hotel lobby and into a locker room. They locked up their personal belongings and were finally told what the surprise was.

Lola booked dolphin experiences for everyone. But only four could go at one time. So, Ricky, Robert, Blair and Lola went first. The others went to the beach for water activities and zip lining.

The first group suited up and met the trainers by the dolphin pool. They each had an hour to spend with their dolphin. The trainers explained the anatomy and physiology of these marine mammals. They did foot pushes, fin pulls and dolphin kisses as part of the experience. The dolphins put on a show with flips and turns for all to see. And they had a little bit of free interaction time with them.

An hour later, the second group suited up as the others headed to the beach to do their water activities and zip lining.

After both groups finished, Lola purchased everyone's souvenir photos and DVDs.

Upon their return, the other two Escalades were parked in front of the lobby. It was time to go shopping. Each couple needed their own truck for their shopping excursion. So, they quickly changed into their clothes.

Mauricio pulled April aside before leaving. He tasked her with a surprise for Lola. He handed her his own credit card to charge the expenses to. Then, he got in the truck and they all left.

Kukulan Plaza was less than five minutes away. In

the brochure, it listed over 250 stores in this plaza. And everyone had maps which made it real convenient.

They all met in front of the Luxury Avenue entrance of the mall.

"Make sure you spend it all or you'll lose it," said Lola referring to the money on the credit card.

Robert wasn't sure what she meant.

Each day their cards would be replenished to equal $20,000. If they saved any money, then the difference would be added. So, they might as well spend it all and get more the next day.

Mauricio, Wyatt and Robert went in one direction while the ladies went in another. Blair and Ricky were off to Fendi and a fuck. Not sure in which order.

Two hours later, their trucks were full. There were bags from Burberry, Cartier, Omega, MaxMara, Ermenegildo Zegna, Mango, Envy, Fendi, Salvatore Ferragamo, Hugo Boss, Carolina Herrera, DKNY and B.you, just to name a few.

Four valet carts were waiting outside the lobby entrance. April and the other assistants had just one more surprise in store for them.

While their bags were being taken to their suites, they went to the spa. Lola booked couple's massages for everyone to enjoy. None of them had been alone with their men all day. So, she thought it would be nice for them to hang out together while getting pampered.

Their services included roses and chocolate full body massages, detoxifying wraps, citric rub exfoliations and pedicure treatments to revitalize the feet.

Mauricio had a surprise for Lola back in the suite. He led her to the bedroom with her eyes closed. When she opened them, balloons covered the ceiling. And there were rose petals in the shape of a heart on the bed.

Then, he led her to the bathroom. It looked like a Sunday church service at a cathedral. There were so many candles lit creating the romantic ambience Mauricio hoped for. It went with the champagne and chocolate bath set-up he chose.

They sat in the tub talking about their day. They shared stories and laughed at their friends.

In the middle of his sentence, Lola just kissed him. He sat her on the rim of the tub and spread her legs open. His appetizer was Lola-a-la-carte.

It was nine o'clock. They had to go. They had a 9:30 p.m. dinner reservation at one of the most exclusive restaurants in the hotel, Kuha Naha Restaurant. They specialized in traditional Mexican cuisine.

Mauricio handed her a jewelry box. It was a 4-carat diamond necklace set with the matching earrings. He helped her put it on.

"Thank you, Baby. This is beautiful," she said touching the necklace.

"You're welcome."

Mauricio escorted Lola to the lobby. Everyone looked like a million bucks. And they most certainly attracted lots of attention as the hostess showed them to their seats.

Everything looked so good on the menu. And they didn't know what to have. So, they explored and shared different authentic dishes, including enchiladas, stuffed tamales, lobster and fish fried tacos and chiles rellenas. They ordered drinks from Margaritas and Piña Coladas to shots of tequila with beer chasers.

After dinner, a trail of waiters came out with a cake singing *"Happy Birthday"* to Lola. Blair and Crystale had a specialty cake made for her. It was shaped like a blue and white Tiffany gift box with edible jewelry hanging from the sides of it. The inside was red velvet cake with cream cheese filling. And the outside was beautifully blinged out.

After dessert, the ladies ran upstairs to quickly change for the club. The men were in awe when they came back down.

Crystale wore a short, red jeweled strapless dress with red heels and silver accessories. Janelle wore a short, halter cheetah print dress with black heels and gold accessories. And Lola wore this short, one-shouldered sparkling silver dress with blinged out heels and diamond accessories.

They ended up at one of the hottest clubs in Cancun, Coco Bongo. This three-story building had a capacity of 3,000. There were three bars on each floor, multi-colored lights flashing everywhere, over 700,000 watts of bass pumping throughout the place and Cirque De Soleil themed servers and entertainment.

Lola and her guests didn't have to wait in any lines. They received VIP treatment as soon as they arrived.

They were escorted inside and to a private VIP area. Four bottles of Cristal awaited them. And the waitress came around taking additional drink orders.

Blair and Ricky left after only forty minutes. They were horny as hell and couldn't hold out any longer.

The others were spread out.

Robert and Janelle sat at one end of the booth kissing and feeling all over each other. Robert slid his finger in Janelle, playing with her. Her body squirmed and moved like she was sexing. After she came, they left.

Meanwhile, Crystale and Wyatt found a storage area behind their VIP area. Wyatt pulled a chair down from a stack. Crystale straddled him. He sucked on her breasts as she rode him. Then, she got up and gripped the back of the chair sexing doggy style. After she came twice, they left.

And while everyone was getting their groove on downstairs, Lola and Mauricio were upstairs. They stood in a dark corner kissing and touching each other. He pulled her onto a nearby table. She leaned forward and cocked her leg up on a nearby chair. The table was rocking as he hit it from behind. Then, he flipped her over and sexed her so good from the front. They left after he came.

Chapter 21
<u>Thursday: Aruba</u>

It was 6:30 a.m. and everyone received a wake-up call. Their flight was scheduled to leave Cancun in an hour. So, they had to hustle. They were just glad they didn't have to pack. The hotel butlers did it for them while they were at the club.

The flight time to Aruba was about four hours. They slept the entire way.

Lola planned the island days pretty much the same. They flew into each destination on a private jet. Individual SUVs picked them up on a red carpet. Each couple had their own personal assistant to help them with activities throughout the day. And only the most luxurious hotel suites for each couple. They drank, shopped, clubbed and experienced fine dining at its best. They enjoyed wild sexcapades. And lots of pictures and videos were taken.

Once they landed, the pilot made the arrival announcement. Everyone woke up a bit more refreshed.

"Ready to do it all over again?" asked Lola chuckling.

"Yep. Let's go," said Ricky. "Party over here..."

As they looked out of the windows, four white Hummer H2s were parked. The excitement began all over again.

This time, they stayed at the Hyatt Regency Aruba. Again, they each had the Presidential Suite with a slew of amenities and services.

Mauricio and Lola loved the openness of their 5,200

square foot room. It was decorated in shades of whites, aquas, greens and oranges. It made the room feel light and airy. And the richness of the Mahogany wood flooring made the room feel warm and cozy.

They all met by the pool a half hour after checking in. They ordered tropical delights with funky names like, Aruba Riba, Summer Surprise, Day at the Pool and Raspberry Ricky. For appetizers, they ordered two of each: crab cakes, Asian chicken wrap, chicken wings, French fries, mini Angus burgers and loaded nachos. Again, Blair ordered shots of Patron and Ricky ordered beer chasers. They got their party started early again.

Next was shopping. Their credit cards had been replenished to equal $20,000. And this time everyone received $1,000 in cash.

Aruba was a refuge for any type of shopper. With duty-free tax, international labels and low prices, Aruba was a shopper's haven.

The Royal Plaza, Renaissance Mall, Main Street and the Village Mall were just a few places they visited and found bargains. They even stopped by Palm Beach Plaza for a game of bowling and more shopping.

They spent the entire afternoon and early evening doing their own activities. These included browsing, swiping, harbor shopping, market place snacking and getting to know the streets of Aruba with each mall in close proximity of one another.

At the end of their shopping excursion, they had been to Gucci, Furla, Louis Vuitton, Diesel, Guess, Ralph Lauren, Cartier, Bulgari, Adidas, Salvatore Ferragamo, Calvin

Klein, Fossil, Bisou Bisou Pink, Aaron Basha, Movado, Roberto Cavalli and BCBG, to name a few.

By the time they returned to the hotel, it was dinner time. They had one hour to shower, change and meet back in the lobby. She had a surprise for them.

Dinner was the special surprise planned on the island. She primarily chose the Hyatt for this feature.

The hotel offered what was called 'Paradise by the Sea'. It consisted of a candlelight dinner for two on the beach. However, Lola arranged seating for eight.

It was the most romantic, relaxing and intimate setting they'd ever seen. A trail of silky red rose petals led to their tented area by the water. Moonlight, stars, candles and Tiki torches provided lighting. And there was a line of uniformed staff waiting to serve them.

As they made their way down to the beach, butlers carried their shoes as the coolness of the sand refreshed their feet. Red roses were given to each of the ladies. A guitarist serenaded them as they were seated. A photographer went around capturing their every moment. And no interruptions from the public occurred as they experienced this private four-course dining extravaganza.

Lola and her guests didn't have to worry about ordering. A set menu was prepared for the evening.

They started with lobster and shrimp crab cakes with honey Dijon sauce, grilled prawns on fried plantains and small cups of roasted tomato soup with shrimp and cream cheese as appetizers.

Next, the waiters served them a cranberry, Mandarin orange and cashew salad with raspberry vinaigrette.

For their main course, they each had two plates to dine from. The first plate had Plantain crusted Snapper with a Papaya Beurre Blanc sauce and a lemon Risotto. The second plate had Pepper-crusted Filet Mignon with a mushroom sauce and a Caribbean grilled lobster tail with a shrimp Creole sauce. It was served with parmesan-garlic mashed potatoes and prosciutto-wrapped asparagus with toasted almonds and honey-glazed baby carrots.

They sat there enjoying their food, ambiance and each other's company.

Dessert wasn't for a while. But when it came, it all looked delicious.

Each evening, the chef prepared specialty desserts. So, the waiters came with sampler trays of the evening's delights, which included classic flan, chocolate Dutch Lava cake, peach and apple bread pudding with caramel sauce and vanilla bean and caramel cheesecake with a white chocolate brandy sauce.

Crystale and Blair also had a small, two-tiered cake made for Lola's birthday. It was an ocean themed cake with white frosting and all kinds of colorful seashells on the outside. The inside was marble fudge with raspberry filling.

On the very top sat a 4-carat diamond bracelet with seashells and dolphins that Mauricio bought for her. She had never seen one like it before.

The evening was without a doubt an unforgettable experience for all of them.

After, they tried their luck at the casino before heading to a club. Lola and Janelle went to the slot machines. Blair, Crystale and Robert tried their luck at Blackjack. Mauricio,

Ricky and Wyatt played poker.

There were big four winners of the night. Crystale won $8,000, Ricky won $7,500, Mauricio won $5,000 and Janelle won $3,000.

Before going to the club, Mauricio handed her a gift box.

"What's this?" she asked.

"Open it."

It was a Louis Vuitton 18K gold diamond heart locket necklace. Their picture was inside. He wanted her to have a keepsake of him when they're apart like she did with her mother. She loved it.

Club Confessions was their last stop. This giant building looked like a warehouse with flashing lights, music pumping and thousands of people.

Chapter 22
<u>*Friday: Turks and Caicos*</u>

Their flight to Turks and Caicos was less than two hours long. So, they were able to sleep in until 8 a.m. Again, the hotel butlers packed their clothes the night before.

Upon their arrival, four white GMC Denalis were parked waiting to pick them up one by one on a red carpet.

Lola's special surprise for this island was the resort they were staying at. Grace Bay Resort was one of the most exclusive and world-renowned resorts in the world.

This romantic getaway had the largest tropical oasis, sat on one of the most pristine beaches and had amenities designed to cater to their guests. Relaxation and individualized attention were this resort's motto.

The resort offered three types of accommodations: the hotel, the villas and the estate. Lola reserved one of the spacious residential penthouses with just over 10,000 square feet in the estate.

The unique feature about this penthouse was the four oceanfront master bedroom suites with their own private master baths and private terraces. This allowed them to stay together while still having privacy.

It also had a full kitchen with a mini wine cellar, an oceanfront living room and dining room, a media room and outdoor steam showers. And the balcony, which overlooked the ocean, wrapped around the entire unit.

Everyone was blown away by its beauty. The main living

space appeared fresh, open and very sophisticated. It was decorated in white with glass or clear acrylic furnishings. Baby blues added softness and delicacy. Freshly cut white calla lilies were everywhere. And there was heated tile flooring all throughout. It was absolutely beautiful.

It was such a gorgeous day that everyone decided to order room service and eat out on the balcony. The sun was beaming, there were blue skies for miles and the view of the ocean was captivating. Its turquoise colored water appeared so refreshing and exhilarating. It reminded Lola, Blair and Crystale of Miami.

After looking at the menu, Lola and Blair ordered conch fritters, fried conch cakes and a conch platter that had coconut conch salad, curried conch and cracked conch. Mauricio and Wyatt wanted to try the fish cakes and beef patties. And Crystale ordered coconut shrimp, quiche and fruit for all to enjoy.

And since they were on a rum kick, they ordered Pink Panties, Naked Ladies, Mojitos, Miami Vices and Lifesavers.

They all decided they wanted to hang out on the beach and do some water activities since they missed out the day before. So, they decided to take advantage of the yacht rental that came with the penthouse.

Lola called her personal assistant, William, to advise him of their plans. However, the type of yacht she was requesting wasn't offered with the hotel room. It would cost extra, but she didn't care. She wanted a big yacht with all the water sports equipment that was available. And she would pay whatever was necessary.

While the yacht was being prepared and fully stocked according to Lola's requests, they went shopping.

Treasure Island was the shopping mall located on the other side of the resort. It was mainly for the guests of Grace Bay Resort, but was open to the public. So, the drive was a short one.

This quaint and charming mall was vey unique. It was built like a maze so that every store on the first, second, third and fourth floor could be visited.

The majority of the merchandise on the first floor was from the locals. Lola and the gang supported them by purchasing custom made jewelry, island clothing and shoes, homemade rum cake, liquor, souvenir T-shirts, handmade hats and magazines.

Then, they went up the maze to stores like Marc Jacobs, Michael Kors, Armani, Cartier, Rolex and Bulgari. They even had specialty stores for women, men and shoes.

Mauricio and Lola stopped at Rolex. He wanted to buy her something really nice. So, they browsed the display cases searching for the perfect one. He told her to pick anyone she wanted. But nothing popped out at Lola.

Then, the store manger showed them his exclusive collection he had in the back. Mauricio saw the perfect one for her and bought it.

Lola also saw a vintage watch she liked for Mauricio. So, she distracted him while she secretly purchased it. His birthday wasn't for another few months, but it could be an extra gift.

They got to the fifth floor. It was reserved for only the most elite guests of the resort. To enter, color coded wristbands had to be worn. And a $10,000 minimum purchase amount was required by each guest.

Lola and her guests had their wristbands on and were ready to shop.

It was like being in heaven and New York at the same time. They found exclusive deals on designer labels like Vera Wang, Dior, Oscar De La Renta, Versace, Chanel, Prada and Dolce and Gabbana. So, they went crazy. They spent over their budget, but Lola took care of the bill.

Three hours later, they returned to the hotel. Their things were taken to their penthouse while William led them to the marina.

They boarded a 249' yacht with a crew of 22. There were eight cabins, a pool and an outdoor garden area on the back of the yacht.

They spent the afternoon tanning, listening to music, dancing, eating and drinking while touring the island of Turks and Caicos. They anchored near the shorelines to do some snorkeling and diving. They also rode on jet skis, banana boats, tubes, paddle boats and did some kneeboarding. And a huge trampoline was inflated for them to jump on and in to the water.

Dusk fell and they were full, tired and drunk. They had eaten and drank so much on the yacht that they weren't hungry. So, dinner was out. And they were active all afternoon, so they just wanted to chill.

They tried their luck at the casino. The big winners of the night were Blair with $15,000 and Lola with $13,500. Wyatt and Crystale each won $4,000. And Robert won $3,500.

Afterwards, they went to the hotel's Infiniti Bar. This massive bar stretched out ninety feet from the resort to the shores of the beach. And all while serving up the largest drinks on the island.

Each couple shared a 36-ounce alcoholic beverage. They ranged from Sunset Mojitos to Raspberry Rum Punch. They talked, laughed and enjoyed the live music while sipping on their drinks and watching the bonfire on the beach.

Chapter 23
<u>Saturday: New York</u>

It was Lola's birthday. She woke up very excited. She could hardly wait to get to New York to see her surprise. The flight time was about four hours. So, they got up early to make their scheduled arrival time of noon.

Lola had to charter a bigger jet back to the States. They had done so much shopping that she needed to make sure their stuff could return with them. She was very conscious of the weight requirements.

On the plane, everyone sang *"Happy Birthday"* to her and toasted her with glasses of champagne. Lola was too excited to sleep. So, they watched videos from the past few days of island hopping. They laughed and talked about it the whole way there.

When they landed, there were four black executive Suburbans parked. And like before, they pulled up to the red carpet one after another as each couple exited the aircraft.

Mauricio reserved the Royal Plaza Suite for his queen at the Plaza Hotel as suggested. It was regal and superbly decorated with Earth tone colors, dark wood flooring and gold trimming that made the room sparkle. Everyone else stayed in the Plaza Suites.

Mauricio arranged for Lola to spend the next few hours getting pampered at the spa. He needed to keep her busy while he finished up some last minute details.

She indulged in services that included a honey and wine wrap, grape bath, stone therapy, cranial massage, a facial, manicure and pedicure. She was very relaxed when she came out of there.

After the spa, Lola had a glam squad waiting for her in her suite. All the ladies, including Blair, got their hair and make-up done.

Lola was almost done when Mauricio came through the door with a big box and some bags. He had several surprises for Lola.

Mauricio started to get ready while Lola and the gals were finishing up. Once everyone left, Lola went to open her gifts.

She opened the biggest one first. Her eyes lit up like a kid in a candy store. It was a beautiful red, satin, strapless two-piece mermaid gown. At the waist, it gathered and was embellished with gold beads, jewels and sequin. It went well with the new pair of red Christian Louboutin You You sling, peep toe shoes and matching satin clutch that he got for her.

"Oh my God! Baby, it's beautiful," said Lola as she changed into it.

"I knew you would like it. Blair helped Camelia design it."

"I love it!"

"It's an original," teased Mauricio.

The dress hugged her body just right.

Then, Mauricio approached her with what looked like a jewelry box.

"This was my grandmother's. I'd like you to have it," he

said handing it to her.

Lola was taken aback when she saw what was inside.

It was a 23-carat gold and ruby necklace set with matching bracelet and chandelier earrings. The necklace was made of flower clusters with ½ carat rubies in the middle of each. Smaller rubies were situated throughout the rest of the necklace making it shine. The bracelet and earrings matched the design.

"I don't know what to say," she said surprised.

"May I?" he asked extending his hand out for the box. She allowed him to put the jewelry on.

"You look beautiful, Baby Girl," he said kissing her on her cheek.

"Thank you, Baby. I mean for everything," she said touching the necklace.

As they walked through the lobby of the hotel, she felt like Julia Roberts in *Pretty Woman*. Everyone looked at them. She was stunning! She grinned from ear to ear walking on Mauricio's arm.

They pulled up to Pier 17. Mauricio escorted her out of the car and down the dock. She saw this beautifully decorated white yacht with four decks and tons of windows. The name on the side said *'Amelia'*. There were balloons and fabric draping all over the outside. And there was a tent on the sky deck.

Photographers and videographers took pictures and videos of her arrival. The guests whistled, screamed her name and cheered her on as she approached the vessel. All she could do was smile and wave.

As she boarded, Blair and Crystale were there to greet

her.

"Oh my God, Lo…You look so beautiful," said Blair.

"You really do," said Crystale.

"Thank you," she said hugging them both.

She saw Camelia and gave her a big hug. She thanked her for the dress and promised to talk business with her later. Esteban and Maritza also approached her. She hugged Esteban as he wished her a happy birthday.

Ana and David couldn't make it. Ana got sick. But David reassured Lola that her madrina would be fine. She went to the doctor and just needed rest. So, although Lola was sad and disappointed, she understood. Her madrina's health was first.

Mauricio helped Lola up the stairs and to the lounge area where the rest of the guests were. It looked like something out of a magazine.

Red sheer panels with strands of gold beading draped the ceiling. Three and four foot glass cylinders contained red orchids, gold rocks and floating candles. There were huge bouquets of floral arrangements including red roses, orchids and mini calla lilies with draping crystals. Red and gold pillows accentuated the white sofas. The u-shape bar had red and gold draping and LED lighting to make it stand out. The bartender even had two signature drinks named Lolatini and Lojito, which she thought was so cute. There were plasma TVs, bling everywhere and red and gold balloons to accessorize. It was romantic and blinged out like Lola liked it.

They departed on time for their six hour cruise around the Hudson River. Uniformed waiters began serving hors d'oeuvres fifteen minutes after departure. Thai shrimp rolls, salmon croquettes, jumbo sea scallops wrapped in bacon, chicken teriyaki kabobs, stuffed mushroom caps with crab salad and lobster bisque were being passed around. Lola tried them all.

Lola went to check out the sky deck. Again, it was beautifully decorated.

On one side, there was a large red Moroccan-type tent with gold frills and trimmings. Red sofas and colorful pillows adorned the inside. And enormous decorative and jeweled pillows were provided for floor seating.

On the other side was the DJ cranking out the music with huge speakers and special lighting effects around him.

And in the center was a photo station for picture taking.

Esteban saw Lola taking pictures. He asked if he could take one with her. She didn't mind and offered to take more than one.

Afterwards, they moved to the side railing and talked.

"You look so beautiful, Lola," said Esteban.

"Thank you."

"The necklace looks beautiful on you. Do you like it?"

Lola touched her neck again. "I love it. It's gorgeous."

"It was my mother's," said Esteban. "Mauricio wanted you to have it. And I agreed."

"Are you sure?"

"Yes, please…Accept it."

"Ok…Thank you," said Lola giving him another hug.

Then, Darlene walked up. Esteban stayed staring at her.

"Hi," said Darlene.

Lola let out a scream as she hugged Darlene tight.

"Happy birthday, Sweetie," said Darlene.

"Thank you, Tía. I'm so glad you came," said Lola.

"Me, too," interrupted Esteban, smitten by her beauty.

Lola properly introduced them after laughing at his boldness.

Darlene was Lola's aunt. She was a white and Cuban woman that stood 5'6" tall with brown eyes and long, black hair. Her light bronze colored skin and small frame had Esteban lost in her presence. She looked like a real-life Pocahontas doll.

"Is Amanda with you?" Lola asked Darlene referring to her daughter.

"Yes, she's around here somewhere."

After about thirty minutes, Blair asked everyone to join him in the lounge. He had a surprise for Lola.

"Well, Miss Thang…You did it again," said Blair.

"What?" asked Lola curiously.

Blair handed her a box. There was an envelope inside.

"Is this what I think it is?" she asked excitedly.

"Yes!!! We got the account. It's official," Blair told her.

They hugged and screamed in each other's ear. Crystale joined them. Mauricio cut in and gave her a big hug and kiss. Then, he explained what all the hype was about to all the guests. They all clapped and congratulated them.

The upper deck opened up and it was a smorgasbord of appetizers with an immaculate presentation.

There were tall bouquets of red flowers on gold planters, lighted columns wrapped in red draping and the staircase had the same red draping with strands of crystals hanging from it. Parlor tables with gold linen and seating for two completed the design of the room.

There were seven food stations with different appetizers at each:

<u>Chilled Seafood</u>: jumbo shrimp, crab claws, lobster tails, oysters and king crab meat.

<u>Sushi</u>: an elaborate assortment of sushi rolls, including California, Spider, Spicy Tuna, Dragon, Rainbow and Shrimp Tempura rolls.

<u>Hot Seafood</u>: coconut shrimp, mini crab cakes, lobster balls, shrimp ravioli and mini lobster tarts.

<u>Fruits</u>: sculpted fresh strawberries, pineapple, watermelon, cantaloupe, mango and grapes.

<u>Deli</u>: cheeses (gouda, cheddar, mozzarella, feta, bleu cheese, Asiago and Brie), veggies (tomatoes, carrots, celery, cauliflower, cucumbers, broccoli and black olives), cold cuts (Prosciutto, turkey, salami, chicken breast, pastrami and roast beef) and breads (sourdough, French, rye, Kaiser, ciabatta and wheat).

<u>Kids' corner</u>: pigs in a blanket, mini meatballs, mini pizzas, mozzarella sticks, mini egg rolls filled with macaroni and cheese and chicken fingers.

<u>Meat station</u>: carved pieces of top sirloin, filet mignon and prime rib.

After a couple of hours of dancing, mingling and drinking, guests were instructed to report to the main deck for dinner.

The red theme followed into the dining area, including red and gold linens, red floral centerpieces with strands of hanging crystals and candles that illuminated the room.

"Can I have everyone's attention, please," said Mauricio

from the middle of the dance floor.

He continued with his speech as Lola stood next to him. Then, he got down on one knee and reached in his coat pocket.

"I love you and I wanna spend the rest of my life with you. Will you do me the honor of being my wife?" asked Mauricio, opening the ring box.

Lola stood there covering her mouth in shock.

"Baby, are you sure?" she asked. "'Cause you can't take it back."

He laughed and said, "Yes, I'm sure. Baby, you're the one."

Full of nerves, Lola said, "Yes…Yes, I'll be your wife."

The audience clapped and cheered as Mauricio slipped the ring on her finger. She kissed him and said, "I love you".

"I love you, too," he said hugging her tight.

Blair and Crystale ran over and hugged her. Robert and Wyatt ran over as well. They were all happy for them.

Lola's ring was a 16-carat, platinum diamond engagement ring. A 12-carat Emerald cut stone sat in the center surrounded by a double micro pavé border. The band had baguettes in a channel setting with micro pavé diamonds bordering the baguettes.

At their private table, Lola just kept looking at her ring. Mauricio kept laughing at her looking at the ring. He thought it was cute. She thanked him for making her so happy. He told her he was only doing what she had already done.

Dinner was kept light since they had tons of food earlier.

Most of the guests dispersed to the sky deck after dinner. Some went to relax in the tent while others went to take pictures and dance.

Lola saw Maritza in a corner with the DJ. He had one hand on her butt and the other on her breasts. Then, Maritza handed him a roll of money. He put it in his pocket and took her by the hand. They went downstairs to the first level. Lola followed them to a bathroom. She overheard Maritza telling Mark, the DJ, how she was going to encourage Mauricio to take Lola's money. That way, he could give her some. Mark requested his share.

Then, the talking stopped. She put her ear closer to the door. All she heard was kissing sounds with moaning, groaning and banging. She knew what was going on at that point and left. She couldn't stomach hearing them anymore. But not before recording everything.

Lola returned to the sky deck a little distraught. And she assumed it showed.

"Are you okay?" Esteban asked Lola.

"Yes, I'm okay," she said smiling trying to hide her feelings.

"Happy birthday, Lola," said Esteban handing her a gift box.

She ripped off the paper and opened it.

"This is too much," she said covering her mouth again.

Esteban gifted her with an 18-carat black diamond necklace. It was one of the rarest black jewels she'd ever seen.

The chain was a single strand of Brilliant round diamonds totaling three carats. But the pendant…this is what made it one-of-a-kind. It was a 15-carat; irregular shaped black diamond surrounded by a micro pavé border of smaller rounds diamonds.

"This is exquisite," said Lola.

"It was also my mother's. Please accept it," said Esteban.

She immediately hugged Esteban.

"Thank you so much for my gifts," said Lola.

"You're welcome, Sweetheart," said Esteban.

Mauricio just watched her. Each time her reaction was genuine. This confirmed what he felt. She wasn't in it for the money.

Since she was a Fourth of July baby, her cake came rolling out with sparklers on it. It was a four-tiered red fondant cake with gold tiaras and edible jewels on each tier. Everyone sang *"Happy Birthday"* to her. Then, the sky lit up with fireworks. They were big and bright; multi-colored and single-colored; and popped out in combination and one at a time. Mauricio held her as they watched.

It was midnight and the evening was over. They docked back at the pier. Most of the young adults were going clubbing. Esteban immediately sent Maritza home with the driver. She was drunk and out of control. Mauricio and Lola decided to go back to the hotel. She really needed to talk to him. Crystale and Wyatt did their thing. So did Blair and Ricky. Darlene was tipsy and couldn't drive. And her daughter, Amanda, wanted to go with EJ to the club. So, Esteban offered to take her home. Darlene accepted. Esteban told EJ to take care of Amanda. Lola asked Esteban to do the same with Darlene.

Chapter 24
Lola's birthday night

Lola walked in the hotel room first. Dozens of red roses filled their suite.

"I wanted your night to end special," he said.

"Thank you, Baby. I love it," said Lola.

Mauricio kissed her passionately holding her close.

"I love you, Baby Girl," he said looking into her eyes.

"I love you, too."

He was excited. The night had gone according to plan so far. And making love to his soon-to-be wife was gonna be the best part of the night.

He led her to the bedroom where rose petals covered the entire bed. He let her hair down and helped her out of her dress. Her beauty mesmerized him. He watched her as he took his clothes off. Then, he picked her up and laid her on the bed. Unfortunately, Lola couldn't get his mother off her mind. And she hated to ruin the moment, but she had to do it.

"Baby, I need to talk to you," whispered Lola.

"Ok," said Mauricio still kissing her.

"Baby, please…" she said completely killing the mood.

"Now?" he asked anxious to be inside of her.

"Yes," she said separating her face from his.

"Baby, can't it wait? I mean I'm about to…" he started to say.

"No, it can't."

He couldn't believe she wanted to talk right then. Things were going so well. But, he stopped, got up and went over to the couch. And he made her get off the bed. It was for love making only, not talking.

"Ok…What's on your mind?" he asked with his dick harder than a jaw breaker.

"Baby, what's the deal with your mom?"

"You wanna talk about that? Right now?" asked Mauricio a little agitated.

"Yes, I do."

Mauricio realized the sooner he cooperated, the sooner he'd get some. So, he took a second and thought about baseball. He figured the faster he got into talk mode, the sooner Lola would get into sex mode.

"Ok…What do you mean, Baby Girl?" he asked more calm.

Lola told him what happened on the yacht with Maritza and what she said. She even told him she recorded her. He was embarrassed, but understood her need to know the truth. But first, he reassured her that he wasn't interested in her money. He didn't need it.

"Baby, my family is goin' through a lot right now. My parents are in the process of getting a divorce. My dad found out that my mom's been cheating on him. And not just recently. For a while now," said Mauricio.

"I'm sorry to hear that, but I think your dad is better off without her. He seems like a really nice guy and deserves to be happy."

"He does. And I hope he finds someone that will. But the thing with my mom is that she only cares about money."

"I'm really sorry."

"And now my dad has to prove her infidelity according to his attorney. If he doesn't, she could end up with all kinds of his money."

"Damn…That sucks. But why does she think you'd help her take mine?"

"'Cause I did it before 'til I found out the truth."

In the beginning, Mauricio blamed Esteban for the problems between his parents. He believed the lies his mom fed him. So to get back at his dad, Mauricio asked him for credit cards, cash, loans and anything of value to give to his mom. But, Esteban quickly caught on to Mauricio's game. He sat EJ and Mauricio down to explain the truth. He showed them pictures, videos, credit card statements and receipts and let them hear recorded conversations. He showed them all the evidence he'd collected regarding their mother's infidelity.

Mauricio was hurt and disappointed in himself for falling prey to his mother's lies. And he apologized to his father, especially after he overheard one of Maritza's conversations.

Maritza planned to use Mauricio the whole time to take everything Esteban had. She also mentioned how she couldn't count on EJ to help her because he was too much like his real father. And she really didn't like either one of them. Mauricio had a hard time believing a mother could say that about her own child.

So from that day forward, he realized three things. First, Esteban wasn't EJ's biological father. Second, he wanted the best relationship two brothers could ever have.

So, he made it a point to love, care and be there for his little brother even more. And lastly, never trust a woman. Never!!!

"That's why I didn't trust females. And why I never gave one a chance. I never wanted to go through the shit my dad is goin' through right now," he explained.

"I understand. Who would?" she questioned.

Mauricio admitted how the situation really affected him. When he first found out about his mom, he thought all women were like her. So, he dogged them out and treated them mean. And if they acted like it was all about his money, it was worse. He knew he had hurt some girls that maybe didn't deserve it and some that did. But he had gotten a bad impression of women from his own mother. And if he couldn't trust her, what made him think he could trust a woman off the streets?

Then, she brought up the crucial topic of money.

"Baby, I hate to bring this up, but we have to talk about it," said Lola.

"What?" he asked.

"Money."

"What about it?"

"Well, we need to know each other's worth. I don't want any secrets between us. And there's something I need to talk to you about before we get married," said Lola a little hesitant.

"Ok…"

"And I love my ring. I do. It's more beautiful than what I dreamt it would be. But honestly, Baby, I'm afraid that you really can't afford it. I'm afraid you bought it trying to compete with my lifestyle."

Mauricio got serious.

"Learn this about me now. I wouldn't give you something I couldn't afford. And I don't have to compete with your lifestyle. You just haven't been fully introduced to mine. You have no idea what I have 'cause I've kept my lifestyle simple. But let's talk about it. We need to know what's gonna be protected anyway, right?"

She knew she had just gotten told off. And felt like a fool for making assumptions. But she was just glad they were on the same page about protecting their assets.

Lola went first. She admitted to being a multi-millionairess. She told him about the companies in her mother's estate that David and Ana controlled. There was the prestigious modeling agency, the well-known skin care line, cosmetics line, perfume line with six fragrances for women and the sexy lingerie line which sold mostly in South America, Central America, Mexico and Europe. The club, Motions, on South Beach was hers. He knew about the restaurant, but didn't know she owned two more. And they just launched a new swimwear line in Brazil.

As far as herself, he knew she was a real estate agent and a flight attendant. But, she also did some modeling for her mother's company. And she confessed winning a combined 46.8 million dollars between the pharmaceutical company and the hospital regarding her mother's death.

Her new ventures were designing the uniforms for airline professionals and launching her own accessories line soon. And she owned lots of real estate that supplied extra income as well.

"Damn! I hit the lottery with you, Baby Girl!!" said Mauricio laughing.

Lola shoved him and said, "Babe, that's not funny."

"Ok…Ok."

However, Mauricio was surprised. He didn't think she had that much money, but he was impressed. She preferred creating her own empire rather than living off her mother's. That said a lot about her.

Next went Mauricio. She knew he was a reputable club promoter. But she didn't know he also owned two barber shops, a tow truck company, three car washes, a car service business, a scooter rental business and vending machines in a corporate office building. He was opening a cell phone store next week, his hair and nail salon was opening in a month and he was branching into event promoting. Esteban helped him grow an investment portfolio worth over eighteen million dollars. He also owned real estate that supplied extra income. And he was his father's heir.

Then, he told her about his father's money. Esteban was a billionaire. He owned several companies that charted yachts, including the one her party was on. He had an accounting firm with exclusive and celebrity clientele. He had an upscale jewelry store, franchised ten gyms and had a hefty investment portfolio including oil. Esteban did major business with Spain and Italy and owned property in both countries. He bought two car dealerships with his sister's husband, Freddie and also dealt in plenty of real estate. And last, Esteban inherited his mother's estate of jewelry currently worth well over one hundred million dollars. That's where Lola's jewelry came from, including her engagement ring.

Lola felt like a real dumb ass for making assumptions about his finances. She apologized to Mauricio.

"You're the only woman who knows the truth about my money. Not even my mom knows what me and my dad have," said Mauricio.

"What do you mean she doesn't know? Where does she think the money comes from?" asked Lola surprised.

"My mom knows about the accounting firm 'cause my dad's family had it when he met her. And she knows he does some investing from time to time that has paid big. But she has no clue about the rest. And she knows I do club promoting. But she thinks I make extra money from flipping properties and doing quick investments like my dad."

"Wow. That's crazy."

"Yeah. She can't know the truth or else she'll try to take his ass to the cleaners."

Not long after, Lola was done talking. It was time to give her man what he wanted. She asked him to carry her back to the bedroom. They got their freak on in a bed of roses.

Chapter 25
Back in Miami

Lola went straight to her godparents' house from the airport. She wanted to check on her madrina. And she wanted to show them her ring. Mauricio accompanied her.

"Well, hello there," said David letting them in and hugging Lola.

"Hi, Padrino," said Lola.

"Hello, Sir," said Mauricio shaking his hand

"So, I hear congratulations are in order," said David.

"Yep. Look Padrino," said Lola wiggling her ring finger.

"Nice! Congratulations to you both," said David hugging Mauricio. "Welcome to the family, Son."

"Thank you," said Mauricio.

"Where's Madrina?" Lola asked David.

"Upstairs in the room."

David invited Mauricio into the family room while Lola ran upstairs to see Ana.

"Madrina, are you up?" asked Lola knocking on the door.

"Yes, Sweetheart. Come in," said Ana.

Lola walked in and hugged her really tight.

"Ok…Now let me see it," said Ana referring to her ring.

Lola extended her hand out.

"Wow! Míja, it's gorgeous. But can he afford it?" Ana asked a little concerned.

Lola laughed and said, "I thought the same thing,

Madrina. But yes, he can."

She told Ana a little bit about his businesses and investments. But didn't mention Esteban's money at all.

Lola lay next to Ana as they continued talking. She told her how Mauricio knew about all her money. And how they had each agreed to sign a pre-nuptial agreement before they got married. They each had a lot to protect. Ana was really surprised, but impressed that like Lola, Mauricio was also very responsible. She liked that.

"So, he really loves you then, Míja," said Ana.

"Yep. And I love him, too," said Lola smiling.

"Oh Míja. I'm so happy for you. And I'm proud of you, too," said Ana kissing her on her forehead.

"Thank you, Madrina. I love you."

"I love you, too."

Ana teared up. She remembered Lola as this little girl. And now she was all grown up. She thought about Natalie and how she wouldn't see Lola get married. But she was glad Lola had finally found a good man.

Ana thought about Lola's ring after she left. There was something familiar about it. But she just dismissed it since she couldn't put her finger on it.

Mauricio took Lola back to his place after they left her godparents' house. He had a surprise for her.

"What did you do?" she asked him.

"What do you mean? You don't like it?"

"I guess. But I didn't ask you to do this."

"I know."

Mauricio had had his sex room cleared out. There was

nothing in there. It was bare. The bed, the pole, the cabinet, the videos, the photo albums, everything was gone. He wanted a clean slate with Lola.

"So, what did you do with everything? 'Cause I know you didn't throw it all out," asked Lola.

"I threw everything away, except the DVDs and the photo albums. I boxed them up before we left and sent them to my dad's new place," said Mauricio.

Lola laughed and shook her head.

"Babe, I have to keep them…Just for a little while. I have to show my son how his dad was a player," he said laughing.

"Yeah, right. You're not showing OUR son none of that shit."

"Yes, I am."

"And what if we have a daughter?"

"She definitely can't see any of that. She'll think bad things about her daddy."

Then, Lola asked about Esteban.

"So, your dad's movin' out?" asked Lola.

"Yeah. He couldn't take it anymore," said Mauricio. "He put up a front for me and EJ for as long as he could, but he's just tired. And we told him to do what he needed to do. We'd support him regardless. So, he put money down on a new spot a few weeks ago. But he just told my mom about it."

"What did your mom say?"

"She's glad he's gone. With their final divorce hearing coming up, she figured they might as well get a head start. But she thinks he's staying at my new place that I'm buying out there," said Mauricio referring to New York. "He can't have anything in his name yet."

"I understand," said Lola.

Then, she looked around the room. "So, what are you gonna do with this empty room?"

"I don't know. Whatever you want. This is your home now too," he said.

"Speaking of, where are we gonna live once we get married?"

"I'm definitely movin' in with you," he said smiling.

"Why?" she asked curiously.

"Baby, I wouldn't make you leave your mother's house," said Mauricio real sympathetic.

"Awww…That's so sweet."

"Besides you have all the toys that come with it. The huge grilling area, the yacht, the big kitchen with a chef, the yacht, the jet skis, and the yacht…"

"Ok…I get it! You like the yacht," she said laughing.

"Yeah, I love it. But I love my place too. So, we can keep it and use it as a getaway. Like from the kids. Or family can use it when they come into town."

"I see you've thought of everything."

"Yep. And speaking of family coming to town, my dad and EJ are coming next week."

Esteban was flying in to see Darlene. Lola was really excited for them. She knew her aunt was a wonderful person and deserved someone like Esteban.

She inquired about their night, but nothing happened. Esteban was a complete gentleman. He didn't want Darlene caught up in all of his mess with Maritza. So, they agreed to be friends for now. But he liked her.

Lola left Mauricio once Robert came. They had to do some work for two LA projects. And she went to meet Blair, Crystale and Darlene at Gorgiano's on South Beach to discuss another real estate project from Blair's parents.

Before they got started, Blair had some news. He and Ricky were over. Blair got busted getting head from some six foot tall, white guy at the club they went to the night before. Ricky caught him and yelled some harsh words before leaving. Blair felt bad and tried calling him, but there was no answer. So, Blair assumed it was over.

"You always do that. It's like you sabotage your relationships when they're going good on purpose," said Lola

"No, I don't," he said.

"Yes, you do. You knew what you were doin' in that club. Just like you knew Ricky wasn't the one suckin' your dick. Why did you do that?" asked Lola pissed off.

Blair got quiet for a moment and then said, "He told me he could see himself with me forever."

"So you panicked? You got cold feet?"

"Yes! Yes, I did. 'Cause forever is a long time. And the only one who came close to that was Ivan!" exclaimed Blair.

"Then fix it, Blair! And stop doing that!" said Lola catching herself getting loud. "I don't want to see you alone. You're too good of a guy. You just need to face your commitment issues. And stop messin' around with other people's feelings," she continued.

"Yeah, Blair. Lola and I are settling down. Now, it's your turn. Or do you want to end up alone for the rest of your life?" asked Crystale.

"No, of course not. But I don't know how to stop being afraid," Blair told them.

Just then, Crystale saw Ivan walk in the restaurant with another guy.

"Don't look now," said Crystale eyeing the entrance.

Everyone looked. It was Ivan.

Lola signaled him over. He greeted everyone, but didn't stay long. He didn't want his date waiting for him. It was evident Blair and Ivan missed one another, but Blair was too prideful to say anything. So, they said their good-byes and Ivan left.

When the food came, Crystale got a little nauseous. She could hardly eat because of the smell. They wondered what was wrong with her.

"You sure you're not PG, girl," said Blair.

"I'm not pregnant, Blair," Crystale said with an attitude.

"How do you know?" Lola asked Crystale.

"I'm just not."

"Ok…" said Lola doubtful.

"Shut up you guys. Besides, I can't be pregnant. Graduation is a month away," said Crystale.

"What does that have to do with anything?" asked Lola.

"Graduating has nothing to do with being a hot ass, Chíca," said Blair.

Crystale didn't want to think about it.

Chapter 26
Re'Olan Island

Darlene and the others left the restaurant and went to the check out the property on Re'Olan Island that they were gonna be responsible for.

What was Re'Olan Island? It was only the most expensive zip code in South Florida. It was a secluded residential community nestled on three hundred acres of tropical paradise. This man-made island housed stylish condos, luxurious waterfront mansion estates and a small resort. Blue skies and blue ocean was this paradise's backyard. Living here was a lifestyle, not just a residential experience.

There were three access roads to and from the island. But the main source of transportation was by ferry. There were five ferry stations readily available for residents and visitors. And ferry service ran every fifteen minutes, 24 hours a day for departures and arrivals.

Re'Olan Island catered to the rich and famous while allowing guests to indulge in State-of-the-Art amenities. Some of those amenities included a fitness center, golf course, day spas, parks, restaurants, boutiques, a bank, grocery store/fresh market and golf carts for residents' use as transportation around the island.

Blair, Crystale and Carla all lived on Re'Olan Island. Lola and Blair's parents owned a penthouse there as well.

Blair lived in the most prestigious sub-division there,

Luna De Oro. It was the single tallest building residing in the very center of the island. Luna de Oro had eighteen floors offering only forty residences and housed the wealthiest. These residences came with over-the-top architectural designs, marble flooring, concierge service, private elevators and golf carts per resident.

However, Blair's parents converted the seventeenth and eighteenth floor into the largest living space on the island. With just over 16,000 square feet between the two floors, Blair's unit was the most extravagant. He'd custom-designed his place to fit his taste and style.

He had six bedrooms, seven bathrooms and an open floor plan. It had a private entry elevator with a mini glass elevator inside the unit. It came equipped with a grand living room, formal dining room, Chef's kitchen, home theater, home studio and garden terraces. He sat on top of the world overlooking his paradise.

Crystale, Lola and Blair's parents owned the only penthouses in the second most prominent sub-division, Aqua Azul. Aqua Azul was comprised of three buildings with fifteen floors in each of them. They were the second tallest buildings on the island with penthouses residing on the top floors.

These four-bedroom, six and half bath homes had 7,980 square feet of high ceilings, stylish architectural components and floor to ceiling windows that overlooked the ocean. Theirs' came with private golf carts and concierge services as well, but only because of who they were.

Then, there were two sub-divisions that housed mansion

estates in each of them. They were Casa Del Mar and Casa Del Paraiso. These estates ranged from 9,000 to 14,000 square feet with at least four bedrooms.

Crystale's sister, Carla and her husband, Bynum lived in Casa Del Mar sub-division. They resided in a 10,000 square foot, Spanish hacienda with six bedrooms and eight bathrooms. It had a private pool with Jacuzzi, a basketball court, plush gardens, a dance room and a slough of architectural details.

Darlene was the broker for the island. She teamed up with Blair's parents and created a lucrative partnership. She was responsible for all real estate transactions that occurred: from purchases and sales to leasing and rentals. Blair, Crystale and Lola were three of her six licensed real estate agents under her brokerage firm in Miami. So, everyone made money and it stayed within the family.

Darlene's new project was Mar Del Reyes. It was a newly constructed sub-division that sat on the southeast side of the island. Three of the four buildings contained one and two bedroom condos. The fourth building contained penthouse units and inimitable domiciles that no other development had…spacious lofts.

These twelve story condo buildings had the same layout. Each floor consisted of five units: two 1000 square foot one bedroom condos, two 2,230 square foot two bedroom condos, and one 2,960 square foot two bedroom condo with a terrace patio.

The fourth building was a bit unique. This ten story building appeared as if it were three buildings connected. The lofts resided in the center with penthouses on each side of them. Each section had a private elevator entryway. The four bedroom penthouses were 4,460 square feet. And the lofts had 6,000 square feet of open space.

Once they arrived, Darlene assigned each one of them a condo building. She took the building with the penthouses and lofts. It stood to make the most money.

They inspected random units and checked out the building's design and layout. All of them were spacious in size with Spanish influences and modern designs.

They all met back up in the loft on the tenth floor to discuss pricing for the investment units. Blair's parents allowed a certain number of units to be purchased at cost. And since Darlene was the broker, they had first dibs on them. These were the units they sold at market value to earn a huge profit.

Darlene and Crystale each purchased a floor in one of the condo buildings. So, they each had five units. Lola purchased a floor and the tenth floor loft. So, she had six units. Blair purchased two floors and three penthouses. So, he bought thirteen units.

Chapter 27
<u>Esteban in Miami</u>

Esteban, Camelia and EJ couldn't believe how hot and humid it was in Miami. It was only 10:00 a.m. and the sun was blazing.

Camelia flew down with them for a meeting Lola set up regarding her clothing line. She also had to begin working on Lola's dress for the engagement party. Esteban was there to see Darlene for business and pleasure. And EJ was there for the ladies.

Mauricio's family was taken to Lola and Blair's office. They arrived in time to see their photo shoot.

Lola was laying halfway on a shirtless Mauricio covered in jewelry from the waist up with sunglasses on. Lots of her accessories surrounded them on the floor. Crystale stood in front of a shirtless Blair covered in jewelry from the waist up as well. She, too, had sunglasses on. And they stood in front of a door with lots of handbags hanging from it. The point was to show off Lola's collection.

When it was over, they all greeted one another with hugs and kisses.

Mauricio noticed Crystale looking a little pale. And she wasn't feeling well either.

"Crystale…You ok?" asked Mauricio.

"Yea, I'm fine," said Crystale lying on the couch.

"No she's not and she won't go to the doctor," said Lola.

Lola pulled Mauricio aside and asked him to go get a

pregnancy test. She thought Crystale might be pregnant. So, he left with E.J.

Meanwhile, the others stayed talking business. Lola gave Camelia the rundown on her upcoming meeting for her new line. Esteban offered to sell an exclusive collection of Lola's jewelry in his store, which she appreciated. And last, they discussed Lola's dress. Lola told Camelia the "must-haves" for it. Blair threw in lots of ideas while Camelia drew out several designs with tons of ways to embellish it.

Then, Esteban asked to speak to Lola alone. So, they went into her office and closed the glass doors behind them.

The view of Biscayne Bay was breathtaking. It sparkled as the sunlight hit the water.

"What a beautiful view," said Esteban.

"Thank you," said Lola.

"So, how are you?"

"I'm good. Just busy. There's so much work to do."

"I understand."

"So, what's on your mind? Is everything ok?"

"Everything is fine. There were just a couple of things I wanted to talk to you about," he said pausing. Then continued, "The first thing I want to say is thank you. Thank you for understanding about the pre-nuptial agreement. Mauricio told me you agreed to sign it."

"You're welcome. And yes…I did. I understand cause we both have a lot to protect. Mauricio has to sign one, too. It's a stipulation of marriage in my mother's will."

"Smart woman."

"Yeah, she was. She never wanted a man to take advantage of me."

"If you don't mind me asking, what happened to her?"

Lola told him the story in detail.

"I'm so sorry to hear that. I know it must have been tough on you and your father," he said.

"It was in the beginning. But I can talk about it now," she said.

"And how's your dad?"

"I never met him. He died before I was born according to my mom. So, it was just us. My mom raised me and dedicated her life to me. We were really close."

"Well, she raised a fine young woman. She would be proud. And I'm sorry to hear about your father, too."

"Thank you, but it's ok. I never met him, so it wasn't that hard on me. But, I know he loved my mother. She used to tell me stories about how they fell in love. She always said *'love hard or not at all'*."

Esteban smiled and said, "Wow…I haven't heard that saying in such a long time."

"Yeah, I didn't understand it 'til now."

They talked a little while longer. Then, he brought up the other thing he wanted to talk to her about. He wanted to pay for their wedding. No matter the cost. He insisted on it. Lola didn't want him to, but gave into his persuasion.

Mauricio came back with the test. Blair and Lola made Crystale get up and go take it. There was a look on her face when she came out of the bathroom.

"It's positive," said Crystale holding the stick.

"Oh my God! You're pregnant! Yayyy!! I'm going to be a Godmother!" shouted Lola with pure joy.

Everyone just shook their heads and laughed at her.

"Crystale, I don't mean to be rude, but is it Wyatt's?" asked Mauricio.

"Yeah, it's his," said Crystale nodding her head up and down. "He's the only one I've been with."

"Are you keeping it?" he asked.

"Of course she's keeping it. She can't get rid of the baby," answered Lola for her.

Crystale couldn't think. She was still in shock. But she agreed to make an appointment to see a doctor. She also needed to tell Wyatt.

That afternoon, Esteban met up with Darlene. They met for lunch at a bistro on Lincoln Road near South Beach. They sat outside on the patio and discussed real estate business. She made her pitch about Re'Olan Island. He liked it so much that he wound up purchasing a total of twelve units: two lofts, three penthouses, one floor with five units and two additional two bedroom units. He even purchased four units for EJ, two one bedrooms and two of the larger two bedrooms.

As they sat there enjoying each other's company, Darlene spotted David. She flagged him down and signaled for him to come over. When Esteban saw him, he stood up and out of no where punched him in the face. David swung back hitting Esteban. They were at it with Darlene in the middle attempting to stop it.

"What the hell is wrong with you!?! He's my brother!" screamed Darlene to Esteban.

"You're the reason Amelia left me!" yelled Esteban to David.

"No, I'm not! She never left you! You left her!" screamed David back.

"I would've done that…NEVER!!!"

"You lying bastard!! You left her to raise..." David started to say and stopped.

"What? Say it! Say it," said Esteban all roused up.

"Sis, I'll talk to you later," said David and left.

Esteban apologized to Darlene for everything. But she didn't want to hear it.

"Esteban, I can't believe you!" exclaimed Darlene as she took off.

Esteban paid the bill and chased after her.

Chapter 28
The Past Resurrecting

Ana was at Lola's house going through pictures for the engagement party. She wanted to do a slideshow presentation of the couple.

Ana sat there engulfed in memories. She even laughed to herself looking at some of them. Lola overheard her as she came down the stairs and laughed at her.

"See you later, Madrina. Have fun," said Lola.

"Ok, Míja," said Ana looking up at Lola.

All of a sudden, Ana froze. She looked like she had seen a ghost when she saw what Lola was wearing.

"Madrina, you ok?" asked Lola.

"Yes, Míja. But where did you get that necklace?" Ana asked with a shaky voice.

"Mauricio gave it to me. Isn't it beautiful?"

"It's lovely. But where did he get it from?"

"His dad. But I'll tell you about it later. I'm late for my meeting. Love you," said Lola kissing her on the cheek and running out the door.

Ana began shaking. She left the mess on the floor and ran home. When she got there, she walked right passed David who was cleaning himself up from the fight he'd just had with Esteban. She didn't even stop to ask what happened. She headed straight for her closet and pulled down a photo box that was tucked away. Inside were pictures and other memorabilia of Natalie, including some with Lola's father, Náto (pronounced Naw Toe).

"Here it is! David...I found it!" she frantically said waving a picture.

"Woman, what's wrong with you?" he asked.

"Look at the picture. Look at what Natalie's wearing."

"Ok."

"Look at the necklace."

"It's nice. What about it?"

"I just saw Lola wearing the same one."

"Ok. It belonged to her mother. What's the big deal?"

Ana explained what the big deal was. Náto gave Lola's mom that necklace years ago. Ana recognized it because she had never seen such a beautiful black jewel in her life. But supposedly Náto snatched it off of Natalie's neck one day when they got into an argument. Náto was supposedly the last one with it. So, how did Mauricio get it? Or better yet, where did Esteban get it from?

"That's the one he snatched that day?" asked David.

"Yes," said Ana.

"Speaking of Náto, I ran into him today," said David.

"What!?!" yelled Ana.

David explained what happened. He was having a cozy lunch with Darlene on Lincoln Road when Náto just stood up and punched him. David couldn't believe he did that.

It was all too coincidental now. Ana wondered how Darlene knew him. And if he was looking for Lola. Ana got scared. David tried calming her down.

"Náto doesn't know of Lola's existence," he said.

"That's not true," she said.

Natalie found out she was pregnant after Náto stood her

up at the altar. But she wanted to see if he would try and make it work with her one last time. So, she sent him a letter, a copy of the ultrasound picture and her engagement ring. He was supposed to come back and put the ring on her finger when he was ready. But he never showed up.

"What if he's using Darlene to get information about Lola?" questioned Ana.

"Darlene isn't gonna tell him anything," said David.

"But what if he's pretending to be someone else?"

"I doubt it."

Then, she suddenly remembered the familiarity with Lola's engagement ring. It was Natalie's engagement ring. She found the picture where Natalie had it on. How was Mauricio able to give her that ring? And who was Mauricio's father?

Chapter 29
Esteban and Darlene

Esteban chased Darlene a few blocks to the beach. He needed a chance to explain himself. He didn't normally behave that way, but he couldn't help himself. He held a grudge against David for over 25 years.

Darlene stopped to listen to what he had to say. He started from the beginning.

Amelia was the love of his life. He would've done anything for her, including marry her. And they were supposed to, but he didn't show up the day of their wedding. He received a phone call that Mauricio was in the hospital very ill. So, he couldn't leave. But the first chance he got, he attempted to make things right. Unfortunately, he was too late.

He told her how he flew to Miami desperately looking for Amelia. He went to her house, but she wasn't there. However, Ana was. And she told him where to find Amelia.

When he pulled up to the restaurant, he saw David and Amelia kissing outside the restaurant. He approached them angrily. Things got heated and it turned into a big fight. Esteban snatched a black diamond necklace off Amelia's neck that he gifted her. He was so mad and hurt and felt she didn't deserve it.

But he loved her and very much. And he wanted her back. So, he went back to Amelia's house later that night. He wanted to apologize and give her back the necklace.

He also wanted to explain what happened with Mauricio and ask for her forgiveness. But when he got there, he saw something he didn't expect to see.

He stood outside her house about to knock on the door when he saw David and Amelia through her window. He opened a red ring box. Her eyes got big when she saw the ring. David took it out and slipped it on her finger. She stretched her arm out to see it from afar. Then, she hugged him full of excitement. So, he left with the assumption David proposed.

Esteban left heartbroken. He knew he had lost the love of his life forever. And he blamed David all these years for stealing her away.

"And you never saw her again?" asked Darlene.

"No," he said.

He told her how he did receive a letter from her. It stated she was moving to Europe. She returned her engagement ring and wished him well in life. That was the last time he heard from her.

After hearing Esteban, Darlene understood his anger. She even thought it was sweet that he defended his love after so many years. But she was confused. She didn't know who that Amelia person was, but he had it all wrong with regards to David.

She explained how David has only proposed and been married to Ana. They got married a few months after they met. Ana's best friend and Lola's mother, Natalie, threw them a wedding. And he has never been with another woman since.

As far as the house he went to that night, it was

Natalie's. She knew because she sold her that house.

And Darlene remembered the night David went over Natalie's to show her Ana's ring. It was the same night David mentioned getting into a fight with Natalie's fiancée at some restaurant. The guy caught them kissing, but it wasn't what he thought. It was also the same night Natalie found out she was pregnant.

Then, it hit Darlene.

"Wait a minute! Are you Náto?" asked Darlene scared it was true.

"Yes. Only Amelia knew me by that name," he said.

"Oh my God! Oh my Lord!" was all Darlene could say pacing feverishly.

Esteban looked perplexed and baffled. That meant Amelia was Natalie. And he'd been looking for the wrong person this whole time. And why didn't Amelia give him her real name? Then, it hit him…Lola! She could be his daughter. That's what David almost let slip out at the restaurant.

"So, that's why you didn't show up that day," questioned Darlene. "'Cause Mauricio was in the hospital?"

"Yes. They didn't know if he was going to make it. He apparently ate some of Maritza's mom's pills thinking it was candy. So, I couldn't leave him," said Esteban.

"Oh my. And the whole time she thought you changed your mind and tried to work things out with Maritza."

"God, no! I never changed my mind. Never! It's just I showed up when I could. And I tried to call, but Amelia… or Natalie wouldn't accept any of my calls. So, I couldn't tell her what was happening."

"Yeah…I remember. She thought you didn't want to be with her anymore."

"But that wasn't the case."

"Well, we know this now, but she didn't know back then."

Darlene knew this was a nightmare. And Esteban just kept asking a gazillion questions about Natalie. She wasn't sure why Natalie told him a wrong name, but she told him everything she knew.

A floodgate of thoughts opened up for Esteban. He had so much on his mind. His main concern was finding out the truth about Lola. And Darlene was willing to help. Lola deserved to know the truth whether good or bad. She needed to know if she was related to Mauricio. There was a marriage at stake. So, Darlene came up with a plan to find out the truth.

Esteban couldn't believe her and David were siblings. She explained how they have the same mother, but different fathers. Their mother was white and her father was Cuban. However, her father raised David as his own son. And he was the only father David knew.

Then, he changed the subject back to Darlene. He reiterated how much he liked her. He hadn't felt a spark like that since Amelia. She admitted to liking him too. But, they were gonna take their time to get to know one another. He was still in a real mess and she had just gotten out of something herself.

Darlene opened up about her recent battle in court with her ex-husband and Amanda's father, Armando. He tried to steal money from her and kidnap their daughter. He also cheated on her and got someone else pregnant during the course of their marriage. Towards the end, he began verbally and physically abusing her. And on top of that, Amanda gave her hell because of the divorce. She assumed it was Darlene's fault why the marriage didn't last. But Amanda eventually saw her father's true colors. Now they had the best mother-daughter relationship ever.

So, she was finally getting her life back on track. Esteban understood. Besides, he wanted to do things right and give Darlene her place. She deserved that. He didn't want them sneaking around like it was something dirty.

As they walked back to their cars, Darlene's phone rang. It was David. He inquired if Náto and Esteban was the same person. She confirmed his fears.

Chapter 30
<u>Crystale tells Wyatt</u>

Crystale went over to Wyatt's house. She wanted to invite him to her graduation and tell him about the pregnancy.

When she walked through the door, she heard the shower. So, she went to the bathroom and peeked in the curtain.

"Hey," said Crystale letting him know she was there.

"Hey," said Wyatt giving her a kiss. "I'll be out in a sec."

"K."

Wyatt got dressed and went to the kitchen. He put the finishing touches on their dinner.

"I wanted to invite you to my graduation," said Crystale handing him an invitation.

"I wouldn't miss it," he said giving her a kiss. Wyatt was proud of her. And he was excited for her becoming a doctor.

He set their plates on the table. She complimented him on presentation. But the food was making her nauseous. So, she got up and went to the couch.

"Baby, come here please. I have something to tell you," said Crystale patting the couch cushion.

"Ok," he said walking over.

"I'm a little scared, though."

"Don't be scared."

She sat on top of him facing him. She wanted to see his facial expression when she told him the news.

"Baby, there's no easy way to say this. So, I'm jus' gonna show you," she said reaching in her purse, pulling out the pregnancy test. She took a deep breath and showed him the stick. "I'm pregnant," she said smiling.

But he became angry.

"Don't play with me like that," he said pushing her off of him. "You ain't pregnant. You're just a liar!!" yelled Wyatt.

"What's wrong with you?" asked Crystale terrified.

"You like playing games with people?"

"I'm not!"

"Anyone can pee on a stick! How do I know you didn't pay someone to do that?"

"I didn't. I wouldn't do that," she said with a crackling voice tearing up.

He stood right in front of her, very close and said, "Get the fuck out of my house with your triflin' ass!!"

He stood there huffing and puffing in her face until she left.

Crystale called Lola crying her eyes out, but she didn't answer. Then, she called Blair. When he picked up, she told him everything.

Blair told her to go home and he would her there. Then, he called Lola until she picked up. He briefly told her what happened. Lola immediately went to Crystale's house. She told Lola everything in detail.

"What the hell's wrong with him?" yelled Lola. "Pero esto no se va a quedar así!"

Lola was mad as hell and went from English to Spanish. She told them that this couldn't stay the way it was.

"And why would you pay someone to pee on a stick?"

questioned Lola. "Is he fuckin' stupid?"

"I don't know, but he had this look of hatred in his eyes Lo," said Crystale crying in a daze remembering the look.

Lola called Wyatt to curse him out. He had no business treating Crystale like that. But Mauricio picked up his phone instead. Lola didn't care. She went off on him too in Spanish and English. He understood her anger and asked her to calm down. But she didn't want to. She was mad as hell and wanted to know what Wyatt's problem was.

He asked if they could meet so he could explain what was happening. She told him to meet her at her penthouse on the island. There, they could talk there. But she warned him that she wasn't done speaking her mind. And Wyatt was still gonna hear her mouth.

Mauricio arrived about an hour later. He didn't like the situation anymore than she did. And Wyatt was completely wrong for how he treated Crystale. He shouldn't have flashed on her the way he did. But after hearing the story, Lola felt bad for Wyatt. It was terrible what was done to him. She didn't understand how someone could be so cruel. But she still didn't like how he scared the mess out of her friend. And he left her thinking she had to raise a child alone. But Mauricio wouldn't let that happen. Crystale had him and Robert for whatever she needed.

"Come on! We have to tell Crystale," said Lola heading for the door.

Mauricio stopped her. It wasn't their place to explain anything. It had to come from Wyatt. But, Lola didn't want her friend suffering that long. Who knew how long it would take him to say something. Mauricio understood, but made a point in his reasoning. So, Lola agreed not to say anything for the moment. But, she warned him that Wyatt didn't have very long before she sang like a canary. Mauricio agreed and would tell her himself, if he didn't.

Then, Mauricio suggested they spend the rest of the evening with Crystale. He wanted to cheer her up.

But when she saw him, she just hugged him tight and balled her eyes out. Mauricio hugged her back and let her cry. He knew she was in pain, but he didn't like the situation because she was with child. Lola and Blair cried watching her. They didn't know what to do for her.

They spent the evening playing board games and eating Chinese take out.

Chapter 31
Crystale's Graduation

Crystale got up bright and early on the day of her graduation. She had an appointment to see her gynecologist. Blair and Lola went with her.

Her doctor conducted a full examination, an ultrasound and drew blood. From her urine sample, her pregnancy was confirmed. From the ultrasound, she was about six weeks pregnant.

Crystale asked for a copy of the ultrasound picture to show the godparents. Blair and Lola teared after looking at it. She really had a baby growing inside of her.

Lola and Blair took a picture of the picture. Lola sent it to Mauricio in a text message. She hoped he sent it to Wyatt.

Crystale asked them not to say anything in front of her parents about the baby at graduation, at least, not yet. She hadn't figured out how to tell them. Her parents believed in marriage before kids. And she didn't quite do it in that order. So, they agreed to keep the secret. However, her sister, Carla, knew.

After the appointment, everyone went to get ready for Crystale's graduation ceremony. It started promptly at 5:00 p.m. And she wasn't gonna be late. She waited a long time for this day.

All of Crystale's family and friends arrived outside the university a little early. They wanted to take lots of pictures of her with and without her gown on.

Crystale looked so beautiful. She wore a one shouldered, ruffled detailing, animal print Cavalli dress with her hair in an updo.

Then, her dad handed her a box.

"Thank you, Daddy, but what is it?" asked Crystale.

"Open it," he said.

Inside was a Bvlgari watch and bracelet set. Each case setting was full of baguette-cut diamonds. They sparkled with every turn of the wrist. She gave her dad a big hug and kiss. She asked him to put it on before dashing off to line up.

The graduation ceremony was nice, but long as they usually are. Again outside the auditorium, pictures were taken. This time, she had her diploma in hand.

Crystale started feeling really ill. She whispered to Lola that she needed to go to the hospital. Lola told Blair. Then, they acted as if they were kidnapping her for a special surprise. Lola promised her parents to have her back in time for her dinner celebration.

Lola called Carla from Blair's car. She told her where they were going and why. She also told Carla not to tell her parents.

Mauricio was already following behind them in his car.

Lola took matters into her own hands. She texted Wyatt the name of the hospital they were going to. Something was possibly wrong with Crystale and the baby. He should know.

When they got there, Crystale was taken right in. They knew her at the hospital. Carla and Bynum arrived shortly after.

Chapter 32
<u>*Crystale at the Hospital*</u>

"Hello Everyone. My name is Dr. Torres," said the female physician.

"Hi…Hello…" said the crowd sporadically.

Dr. Torres asked Crystale a bunch of questions to formulate a list of her symptoms. They included vomiting, nausea, dizziness, fatigue and weakness. They also discussed her diet.

"Well, I need to conduct a pelvic exam now," said the doctor.

"I'm out…See ya," said Mauricio and Bynum, respectively.

The girls laughed as they exited the room.

Then, the door swung back open. It was Wyatt. He had flowers in hand.

"What are you doin' here?" said Carla viciously.

"I told him to come, Carla. They need to talk. Come on," said Lola making everyone else get out the room.

Wyatt thanked her as she closed the door behind them.

"Is it okay that he's here, Crystale?" asked Dr. Torres.

"Yes. He can stay, doctor. Thank you," she said.

Dr. Torres discovered some very light spotting while checking her and didn't want to take any chances. So, she ordered some blood tests, a urine sample and another ultrasound to check on the baby.

Crystale's nurse was buzzed in to draw blood and get

her urine sample. He also hooked her up to an IV per doctor's orders. According to her symptoms, it sounded like Crystale was dehydrated. So, Dr. Torres ordered fluid replenishment.

Since they had to wait for the lab results before doing the ultrasound, Crystale and Wyatt had time to talk.

"Hi," said Wyatt trying to feel her out.

She didn't respond. She looked the other way. He walked over by the window and grabbed the chair. He pulled it right beside her and sat down.

"These are for you," he said trying to hand her the flowers.

Crystale didn't budge. So, he laid them next to her.

"I'm so sorry, Crystale. And I don't blame you if you never talk to me again. I messed up. And I messed up bad. But you need to know why I lost it when you told me you were pregnant. And I know it doesn't excuse my behavior, but hopefully it will clear up my reasoning for it," he said.

Crystale just looked at him and started crying. Wyatt's eyes teared as he wiped her tears. He told her that he loved her and the baby. And he really wanted to be a part of their lives. But his reaction to her pregnancy wasn't because he didn't want one. It was the total opposite. He wanted one so bad. He wanted to get married and have a family. And he would do anything to have that.

It was just that he flashed back to a time when he heard those same words and was shown that same stick. He got very excited, but only to be disappointed because it was a lie. He couldn't handle that kind of disappointment again.

Wyatt told her the story.

Wyatt dated this woman named Tammy. They were together for almost a year. He thought things were getting pretty serious between them. So, he expressed his desire to have a family and get married. She assured him she was ready and wanted the same thing.

One day, she went to his house and did exactly what Crystale did. She opened her purse and pulled out a home pregnancy test. It showed positive. He immediately proposed. She accepted. They went shopping for her engagement ring and he bought her a brand new car. His parents even purchased them a family home. He was setting her up for a better life.

Then, he started noticing things. She wasn't displaying any signs of pregnancy like sleepiness, nausea, vomiting, cravings, crying…nothing. Her doctor appointments always seemed to fall on days he had to be in court. So, he couldn't go with her. He never saw the paperwork confirming her pregnancy either. And he worried about her working and going to school too much. But the biggest and obvious suspicion was she had no baby bump after several weeks.

So, he did what he knew to do. He got his sisters, Winter and Wonder, on the case. He knew they would found out everything, since women always do when they're being nosey. And they did.

They found out that Tammy had an apartment near downtown Fort Lauderdale. She went there everyday and spent time with different men, who frequently visited her unit. She was seen drinking and popping pills with some of these guys in the parking lot. And they always handed her money before leaving. That left one assumption.

They dug a little deeper and found out that she'd been arrested for prostitution, drug possession with intent to consume, credit card fraud and trespassing. Wyatt wondered what happened because she had a clean record when he checked her out when they started dating.

Then, it got ugly. Wyatt followed her to a house down in Pinecrest one afternoon. He wanted to catch her himself.

He saw Tammy walk inside a nice two story home. Twenty minutes later, she came out in a robe and was kissing on some man. Wyatt jumped out the car and ran over towards them. He began screaming and yelling at her. The guy jumped in between them yelling back at Wyatt. But then, Wyatt froze when he saw her stomach. She was pregnant…like really pregnant. The woman he saw in the morning didn't look like that. So, he wondered who this woman was that looked identical to Tammy with a big belly.

Tammy, her twin sister, Taylor, and two men came running out of the house when they heard the commotion. Tammy and Taylor froze when they saw Wyatt. And Wyatt was speechless to find out they were actually identical triplet sisters.

Tammy was busted and had to explain everything.

Tara was Tammy's pregnant sister. She was four months with twins. Tammy asked her to take a pregnancy test, telling her it was for a friend that was seeing a married man and wanted out of that situation. Tara didn't know Tammy was gonna use it to deceive someone for her personal gain. If she'd known, she wouldn't have done it.

Taylor was the one he took shopping for the ring and

Tammy actually picked out the new car.

Tammy admitted she wasn't going to school in the daytime or bartending at night like she told Wyatt. She was actually a call girl and Taylor was the real bartender. Wyatt couldn't believe how deceitful they'd been.

There was more. Taylor explained to Wyatt how she used his name and money to clear her criminal record. Tammy used her name when she got arrested. That's why he didn't know about Tammy's criminal history until recently.

And on top of it all, Tammy and Taylor were already married. Their husbands were the ones that came running out behind them. Tammy's husband was her pimp. So, she never intended to marry Wyatt.

Wyatt apologized to Tara and her husband before leaving, who were also very apologetic for what happened.

"Damn! That's fucked up. Did you get your stuff back?" asked Crystale.

He did get the ring and the car back. He sold the house his parents bought and purchased his current home. And they paid him back every cent they took.

"They just paid you back…Just like that?" questioned Crystale.

Wyatt hesitated. He didn't want to tell her how he had gotten his money back. And lucky for him, he didn't have to. A female ultrasound tech came in wheeling the machine behind her. Wyatt was glad he escaped that question.

"Hi. I'm Pam. Are you Crystale Harris?" asked the woman.

"Yes," she said.

Pam checked her bracelet just to make sure. Then, briefly

went over what she was about to do.

Wyatt grabbed her hand as gel was squeezed on her stomach. He saw his baby inside of her. He was filled with so many emotions.

"Everything looks good. The doctor will be in shortly to discuss the results with you," said Pam.

"Ok…Thank you," said Crystale as she exited the room.

"Marry me," said Wyatt.

"Marry you? After what you just did to me? I mean it's terrible what happened to you and what she did. But you hurt me and you…"

"Baby, I know. And I'm…" he said interrupting.

"Please listen. You not only hurt me real bad, but you scared me. The look in your eyes that night killed me. It was like you hated me. I thought you were mad because I was pregnant or trying to trap you," she said crying again.

"That wasn't it," he said.

"I know now, but you took something out on me that I had nothing to do with. And I didn't deserve that. I've never been treated like that. Never!"

"Baby, I'm sorry. And I promise it will never happen again. NEVER! You and this baby mean the world to me. I can't lose you. I just can't," he said crying. "You two are my family now."

Crystale just cried.

"Please give me another chance…PLEASE," he begged.

"Wyatt, I love you. And yes, I will give you another chance. But you can't do this to me again…EVER!"

"I promise," he said pulling out a ring box from his jacket pocket. "So, will you marry me?" he asked opening the box.

It was a 6-carat diamond, platinum ring. The center stone was a 4.5-carat, radiant cut diamond with a triple split shank of round diamonds in a pavé setting.

"You remembered?" she said covering her mouth.

"Of course I did. I bought it the same day we saw it," he said slipping it on her finger. "You loved it so much. And I knew then I wanted to marry you. It was just too soon to give it to you,"

He kissed her again and again.

By this time, everyone came in clapping, whistling and congratulating them. They saw him slip the ring on her finger through the little window on the door.

Then, her door swung open again.

"Crystale Anisse Harris!!!" screamed her mother, Evelyn, walking through the door.

There was dead silence.

"I can't believe you! And you…" said their mom pointing at Carla. "How dare you not call me?!"

"I'm sorry, mom. But we didn't want to worry you," said Carla.

"Too late for that," said Evelyn.

"You really scared us, Crystale," said her father, Xavier.

"How did you guys find out we were here?" Carla asked her mom.

"Debra called me to find out what happened to Crystale."

"I guess that's one of the benefits of working at the hospital, huh? Everyone knows you," said Crystale trying to lighten the mood.

Crystale apologized to them profusely. She told them

about her pregnancy and showed them her engagement ring. Evelyn was elated about being a grandma and planning another wedding. But she didn't like being kept in the dark about Crystale's condition.

Xavier shook Wyatt's hand and welcomed him to the family. Then, turned to Crystale and told her how Wyatt stopped by three days ago to ask for her hand in marriage. She was speechless.

When the doctor came in, there were too many people in the room. She ordered everyone out, except Wyatt.

Her test results were fine. The ultrasound looked good. And she wasn't losing the baby. The spotting was just that, but she should return if she started bleeding heavy.

It appeared she was dehydrated likely from all the vomiting and was just experiencing the symptoms of pregnancy. Dr. Torres recommended she take her pre-natal vitamins and prescribed her a medicine to help with the morning sickness. Wyatt assured the doctor he would take care of her.

"I'm really gonna be a dad?" Wyatt asked Crystale once the doctor left.

"You are, Baby. You're gonna be the best dad ever."

"I love you."

"I love you, too."

Chapter 33
<u>News</u>

"I'll get it," yelled Wyatt from the kitchen.

He opened the front door.

"Hey," said Lola, Mauricio, Blair and Ivan at staggering times.

"Hi guys," said Crystale. "Hey, Ivan. Nice to see you again."

"Likewise," said Ivan giving her a big hug. "And congratulations."

"Thank you," she said smiling.

Everyone stopped by Crystale's because she and Wyatt had some big news. And apparently she wasn't the only one.

"Here, Baby," said Wyatt handing Crystale a glass.

"Thank you."

"What is that?" asked Lola.

"It's a protein shake with fruits, soy milk and other healthy stuff," said Crystale.

"Damn, Dawg…That looks good," said Mauricio.

A few minutes later, Wyatt came back with shakes for everyone.

"So what's this big news you have for us?" asked Blair.

Wyatt sat next to Crystale.

"Well…We're gonna have a baby," teased Wyatt.

Everyone laughed and made a joke of it.

"Wyatt and I bought our dream home here on the island,"

said Crystale.

"We're having some upgrades done, but it should be ready by the time we're married," added Wyatt.

Lola and Blair let out screams.

"So you decided on a date?" asked Lola.

"When's the wedding, Biatch?" asked Blair.

"In about four weeks," said Wyatt excitedly.

"WHAT!?!" yelled Blair and Lola at the asme time.

Crystale reminded them of their dream weddings they've planned since high school. They each would have the perfect dress, venue and man. And none of that included kids. So, she wanted to get married before her belly got too big. She was determined to fit into her perfect wedding dress.

"Celine and Marc here we come," said Lola.

"What is that?" questioned Wyatt.

The three of them planned to walk down the aisle to their favorite Celine Dion song. Then, they would dance their first dance to their favorite Marc Anthony song. Wyatt didn't mind Celine Dion. But Marc Anthony wasn't happening. He knew the song they were already dancing to.

Evelyn hired Crystale's wedding planner. And they'd just got word that their venue was confirmed. Now, Crystale had to get fitted for her dresses and take care of the details at the venue. She needed to get as much done before Lola's engagement party this coming weekend.

"When are you going to do all of that?" Lola asked Crystale.

"Tomorrow. I have to do my dress fittings. And after, meet Patricia, my planner, at my location site."

"Well, we're going with you. We need to get fitted for our stuff anyway," said Blair.

"Ok," said Crystale.

"I can't believe you're getting married before me, witch," said Lola jokingly.

Wyatt asked Mauricio to be his best man. Mauricio gladly accepted. And they, too, planned to get fitted for their tuxedos in the morning.

Then, Lola told Blair to spill the news about him and Ivan. Ivan laughed and sat back as Blair told the story.

It happened the night Crystale went to the hospital. Reality sunk in for him. Lola and Crystale were getting married. They now had other priorities. And yes they would always be there for one another, but it didn't mean they would always be available.

Two things really hit him. First, he didn't want to be alone forever. And second, who would take care of him when his girls couldn't?

Blair thought about what he wanted in a relationship. He needed someone he could count on, someone to balance him out and someone who could genuinely deal with his fits and demands. The only person he could think of was Ivan. So, he called him and asked to meet. Blair apologized for any wrong doing and explained his commitment issues. Ivan was willing to work with Blair because he loved him. But, he put his foot down this time. Blair had to change if he wanted Ivan back. They weren't just dating nor doing booty calls anymore. Ivan had to be fully included in Blair's life. That meant equal importance as his two best friends. They had to officially move in together, get to know each other's family, share bank accounts and build a future together. So that meant Blair had to face his fears.

Crystale and Lola were impressed. First, that Blair had actually admitted he was wrong. Then, with Ivan for demanding his place.

"I'm so happy you did that Ivan," said Lola. "He needed a good kick in the ass to wake him up."

"Yeah, I had to. I know Blair is stubborn and likes his way. But I'm not a toy. And I love him…Like I really am in love with him. But he couldn't keep treating me the way he was," said Ivan.

"You definitely know how to handle him," said Crystale.

Then, Blair started to talk about their make-up sex, but Mauricio and Wyatt stopped him. They couldn't stomach that. They respected him and his lifestyle, but that was a bit much for them to hear.

"So, I'm officially off the market, Ladies," said Blair to Lola and Crystale.

They were so proud of him.

Then, Ivan asked Blair, "Can I tell them?"

"Yeah."

The day after making up, Blair went out and bought Ivan a brand new red Jaguar XK. He gave Ivan a key to his condo, opened a joint account and took him on a shopping spree. Blair let all of his guards down and promised to be honest with Ivan at all times.

After all the news, Wyatt invited everyone to see their new house. They purchased a 12,000 square foot mansion estate in Casa Del Paraiso subdivision.

This multi-leveled seven-bedroom, ten-bath home

sat on a corner lot. Its European and contemporary style complemented the rustic elements like their ten foot wooden front door. It had a castle feel to it, which is what Crystale loved about it. It came with an oversized master suite, open kitchen into the family room, vaulted ceilings, three fireplaces, a home theater, a game room and a servants' quarter in the rear of the house. A mini tropical jungle surrounded this oasis. It had a four-car garage and a pool with a waterfall and Jacuzzi. They also had a space at the marina for a small boat.

Wyatt took Crystale to the garage. When he raised the garage door, she screamed.

"You needed something for you and the baby. Do you like it?" asked Wyatt as Crystale hugged him with excitement.

There was a brand new black BMW X5 parked inside with a bow around it.

"I love it," said Crystale kissing him all over his face.

Wyatt gave Mauricio the thumbs up.

"What was that for?" asked Lola.

"I went with him to pick it out. He wasn't sure she'd like it," said Mauricio.

Chapter 34
Lola's Engagement Party

Ana paced Lola's floor. She was nervous about the party. She was nervous about seeing Náto. It meant facing the truth.

"Mujér, stop pacing," said David in a low voice so Lola wouldn't hear.

"David, I'm scared. You know what this will do to her," said Ana frantically.

Just then, Lola started making her way down the stairs. She looked like a Goddess.

"Míja, you look so beautiful," said Ana tearing up.

"You sure do, Sweetheart," said David.

"Thank you, Madrina and Padrino," she said.

David helped Lola down the rest of the stairs while Ana answered the door. It was Mauricio. When he saw Lola, he just stared at her with such admiration.

"Baby, you look so beautiful," said Mauricio taking her hands. "You look like an angel."

"Thank you, Baby," she said kissing him. "You look sexy yourself."

Lola wanted it to be known she was the bride-to-be. She wore a detailed white Gazar organza dress. The bodice was sleeveless with a high collar and a deep V-cut neckline. Chunky floral appliqué detailing added texture and depth. Swarovski crystal beading added that extra sparkle. The full, but flowing multi-layered, ruffled skirt had a sweep train. White Jimmy Choo heels completed the look.

Lola wore lots of carats. Her necklace alone was a 30-carat, platinum, tapering cluster necklace with round, oval and pear-shaped diamonds. She wore the matching pendant earrings and bracelet.

Mauricio looked like a million bucks too. He wore a custom made, white Hugo Boss suit with a black shirt, belt and dress shoes. His tie and cufflinks had white and black in them. And he too wore lots of carats.

His "black ice" was the preference of bling for the night. Four-carat, black diamond stud earrings adorned his ears. He stunted a 30-carat black diamond Arctica watch. He finished off his bling with a 10-carat black and clear diamond bracelet.

It was the best night ever in South Florida. Lola was throwing the biggest bash of the evening…Her engagement party. With over 300 invited guests, the Westin Diplomat in Hollywood, Florida was the place to be.

As Mauricio and Lola pulled up, there was Hollywood-style search lighting outside. Photographers and videographers awaited their arrival. A pink carpet was rolled out instead of a red one. And guests surrounded the entrance area to get a glimpse of the couple.

Lola chose a Moroccan theme for the party. She loved the rich, bold colors that added vibrancy to any room. And she wanted it to be fun with lots of bling, elegance and style.

As Mauricio escorted his lady inside, gold draping canopied the entry way. Photographers snapped lots of pictures. Everyone clapped and cheered once they appeared. They felt like celebrities.

Lola was blown away by the room's sparkle and glam. It exceeded all of her expectations.

The room looked like an enormous tent. Multi-colored panels, Swarovski crystals and rope lighting draped the ceiling, connecting to a huge crystal chandelier in the center of the room. Life-size pictures of the couple stood against the walls near the entrance. Balloons filled the space. There were lots of food stations, floral arrangements, romantic uplighting, candles and lighted furniture. The DJ booth had special lighting and smoke effects. A slideshow of Mauricio and Lola played. And the bar…it was the highlight of the room.

The large C-shaped bar was made completely of ice. Ice chandeliers hung from above. Tall ice sculptures stored bottles of liquor for shots. Lighted spandex columns added color. And everywhere they looked, it was lit up.

But the most impressive piece was behind the bar. There were giant carved ice letters that spelled 'Mauricio & Lola' with colored lighting shining through them.

"Damn, Baby Girl…You out did yourself," said Mauricio.

"I know," said Lola modestly. "You like it?"

"I love it."

Their friends bombarded them with hugs and kisses.

Mauricio saw Esteban and Darlene in one of the lounge areas. So, they went over to greet them.

"Wow! You two look amazing," said Esteban standing up to hug them both.

"Thank you," said Lola.

"Thank you, Papí," said Mauricio hugging him.

"Lo, you look absolutely stunning, Míja," said Darlene giving her a hug. "And you…" she said pointing to Mauricio. "You better be glad I'm taken."

They all laughed.

Then, Lola said, "I see my godparents. I'll be back."

Lola escorted them over to meet Esteban. She was glad they were finally meeting.

"Esteban, I'd like you to meet my Godparents, Ana and David Leon. Madrina, Padrino…This is Mauricio's father, Esteban Hernandez," said Lola.

"Hi. Nice to meet you," said Ana shaking his hand, trying not to be obvious.

David shook his hand, too.

Lola and Mauricio left with their friends, leaving them to talk and get to know one another. But Ana already knew him.

"So, it is you?" she asked Esteban horrified.

"Yes, it's me. And what the hell is going on, Ana?"

"Watch the way you speak to my wife, Náto," said David interrupting.

"I'm sorry, David. But put yourself in my shoes."

"I prayed this wasn't true," Ana said in a low voice, sitting down.

It was the moment of truth between Ana and Esteban.

"Ana, please tell me what's going on. I find out that Amelia lied to me about who she really was. I possibly have another child who thinks her father is dead. And there's a possibility my kids want to marry each other," he said pacing with resentment in his voice. Then said, "And why does Lola think her father is dead?"

"Amelia told her that so she wouldn't look for you. She didn't want to cause Lola any pain. And she never lied to you. You knew who she was. You were actually the only man who knew the real her and who she ever gave her heart to. She just told you her middle name. That's the name she went by at that time. Amelia never used her real name until after she had Lola and started building the businesses."

"Why would knowing me cause Lola pain?"

"Amelia had her reasons why she felt that way."

"What were they? Ana…Please?" he asked sitting next to her.

"I can't tell you that. At least not before explaining everything to Lola. But why did you give her a fake name? Náto isn't your real name."

"I didn't. She knew my real name. She just preferred calling me by my nickname."

"And I couldn't believe you never came back after she told you she was pregnant."

"What?! I wouldn't have NEVER done that! I didn't know she was pregnant. She never told me."

"Yes, she did. She wrote you a letter. It was at the same time she sent the ring back. You obviously got the ring."

"I received a letter from her saying she was moving to Europe with someone she met. And returned the ring. I thought she left with David this entire time."

"What are you talking about? She read me the letter she sent you. She sealed it in front of me. Then, we walked it to the mailbox together. She prayed you would come back."

"Ana, I honestly don't have any idea what you're talking

about."

They each shared their side of the story. It turned out to be one huge misunderstanding.

Then, Darlene told Ana and David what she did. She stopped by Lola's to discuss some real estate business. While there, she took hair samples from her brush. Esteban provided a hair sample as well. She sent it off for paternity testing. The results came back and she sent her assistant, India, to get the envelope from her office.

Ana was furious and didn't like what she did. But understood the need for it.

"I'm scared, Náto," said Ana.

"I am too, Ana. There's just so much," said Esteban.

Meanwhile, Lola and Mauricio were out mingling in the crowd. All of Mauricio's family came down from New York except Maritza. Blair's family came from Brazil. All of Crystale's family was there. Some big name fashion designers, models and PR reps were in attendance along with some famous music artists, producers and athletes. It was a star studded event.

Lola and Mauricio made their way to the dessert table. There were three chocolate fountains as the focal point, serving milk chocolate, white chocolate and pink-colored chocolate. There were towers of different flavored cupcakes and cake dots. Mini cheesecake squares, candied apples, brownies, marshmallow cookies lollipops and guava and cheese pastries were all included in the presentation. And there were mini shot glasses of tres leche (three milk pudding).

They snuck into the dining room area for a sneak peek.

Again, they were blown away.

The room was elegant, but colorful and fun. There were tons of Swarovski crystals, fabrics and frills hanging from the ceiling. The tables and chairs had four major color schemes throughout the room with designer linens and chair covers. Gold charger plates and silverware adorned the tables. Candles with gold ribbon and rhinestones illuminated the room. Large floral arrangements added bursts of color. And there was a variety of fun centerpieces on the different tables, including tall branch trees with mini feather boas, large plume feathers mixed with a floral arrangement and Paillette lamps.

Their area was tented and lit up in fuchsia and red with acrylic furniture. Flowers, feathers, large sparkly pillows and candles accessorized the area.

During dinner, Lola and Mauricio chose their wedding party. One by one they asked their friends and family to be in their wedding. Crystale was her maid of honor while EJ was his best man.

India came back with the letter and discreetly gave it Darlene. She, in turn, gave it to Esteban. He looked at Ana and allowed her to open it. He felt she had more rights.

After reading the results, it was confirmed. Lola was Esteban's daughter. She gave Esteban the letter to see for himself.

Chapter 35
The Truth

Lola and Mauricio were very happy. They were pleased with the party and its turn out. They talked about it all the way to Lola's house. But they had no idea what was about to go down.

"Míja, is that you?" asked Ana as she heard the door.

"Hey," said Lola as they came around the corner.

"Papí? What are you doing here?" asked Mauricio surprised.

"Well, we all wanted to talk to you both," said Esteban nervous.

"I know it's late, Míja, but it can't wait," said Ana.

"Is everything ok, Madrina?" questioned Lola.

"No. No, it's not."

Lola immediately assumed bad thoughts.

"What's wrong? Are you ok? What's goin' on? Madrina, talk to me! You're scarin' me," said Lola raising her voice and tearing up.

"Lola…Mauricio…Please sit down," said David.

"Padrino, is Madrina ok? Did something happen? Is she gonna die?" asked Lola as tears fell from her face, scared at the thought of losing her too.

"No, Sweetheart. No one's gonna die," said David hugging her, trying to comfort her. "It's not like that. But what has to be said is important."

"What's goin' on, Papí? What do you have to do with

this? And why is everyone acting like something bad happened?" asked Mauricio getting worried.

They all felt bad about what was about to happen. But they had to tell them the truth. "Míja, there are some things you need to know about your mom," said Ana reaching for Lola's hands.

"My mom?" asked Lola really thrown off.

"I don't know how to say this," said Ana tearing up.

"Madrina, habla ya!! Talk already," Lola said upset because of the procrastination.

Ana began from when she saw Lola wearing the black jewel. She explained it was one of the rarest black diamonds in existence. It was the only one of its kind with its shape and size. And Ana recognized it because only one other person ever possessed it, that she knew of…her mother. Ana took a half ripped picture out of her purse and showed Lola. Lola was surprised to see it on her mom.

"Madrina, I don't understand," said Lola confused.

"Your father gave it to your mother as a gift. But after an argument, he took it back."

"So, how did you get it dad?" asked Mauricio.

Ana reached in her purse and slowly handed Lola the other half of the picture. Lola put them together and got a good look at her father. He resembled EJ.

"Papí, that's you! You have the same picture of yourself at the house," said Mauricio shocked.

"Yes, Míjo. It's me," said Esteban.

"WHAT!!!!" said Mauricio and Lola jumping out of their seat.

Lola just shook her head side to side. "No! No way! My

father's dead! You can't be him!" yelled Lola pacing the floor with a flood of tears rolling down her face.

"Papí, what the hell's goin' on? You're Lola's father? So, she's my sister?" yelled Mauricio pacing the floor too.

"It appears that way, Mijo."

"How can this be? And you guys knew about this?" Mauricio questioned mad as hell.

"No! No one knew Lola was my daughter for certain until today. We just found out," said Esteban.

"But you acted like you didn't even know each other at the party," Lola told Ana.

"I had to be certain before saying anything, Míja."

"But my dad's name is Náto, not Esteban."

"Turn the picture over, Míja," said Ana distraught and crying.

The back of the picture had "Amelia and Náto" on it.

"Madrina, you knew? You knew this whole time and never said anything to me. How could you? How could you do this to me?" questioned Lola getting louder.

"Lola, I didn't know he was your father 'til tonight," said Ana. "I swear."

"You're a liar! I don't believe you!" yelled Lola at the top of her lungs. "You still knew that my father might be alive and not dead!"

"I didn't know for sure what happened to him. But yes…I knew the possibility of him being alive existed," confessed Ana.

Then, she showed her the letter with the DNA results.

"And how did you get my DNA to do testing?" questioned Lola again, but furious.

"I did it, Lola. I got samples of your hair the day I came over to…" Darlene started to explain.

"Tía, you knew about this, too?" asked Lola surprised. "And came to my house and stole from me! It was my hair! You had no right!" yelled Lola making Darlene cry.

"I'm sorry, Lola. But I was trying…" Darlene started to say again.

"You were trying to what…Help? You thought if I knew the truth that I would what…Be grateful to you and run into my daddy's arms? HELL NO! He is the father of the man I'm madly in love with and SUPPOSED to marry! And now it turns out that I'm his child. So the man I'm in love with is my brother! Do you hear how that sounds? MY FUCKIN' BROTHER!!!" continuously yelled Lola.

"What I don't understand is how none of you said anything. Not a word. If you had suspicions, someone should have said something to us. Instead, y'all continued to let us plan a wedding knowing she might be my FUCKIN' SISTER!" yelled Mauricio angrily, hurt and sad all at the same time.

Needless to say there were a lot of emotions running high in the room.

"Please let us explain," said Ana.

Lola threw her hands up.

Chapter 36
Their Stories

Ana told Natalie's story.

Natalie met Esteban one day leaving a photo shoot. It was love at first site according to Natalie. He invited her to dinner that same night. When she returned from her date, Ana remembered Natalie repeating how cute he was and how he was the one. Well, that date eventually led to a marriage proposal months later when Esteban flew Amelia up to New York.

"Coney Island," said Lola remembering the story Esteban told them.

"Yes, Lola," said Esteban.

Natalie accepted, of course. However, the issue was Mauricio's mom. She wanted Esteban for herself. So, she did whatever she had to in order to tear them apart. But it never seemed to work until Esteban didn't show up for their wedding. That was the last straw.

"Because Mauricio got sick," said Lola.

"How did you know that?" asked Ana.

"I told her," said Esteban. "The weekend I met her we went to Coney Island. I briefly told the kids about my love story with Amelia. And I told them why we didn't get married."

Natalie was so hurt and disappointed. That's why she didn't pick up when he called. She didn't want anything to do with him. So, she never found out Mauricio was in the hospital.

Then, she found out she was pregnant and had to face the truth about loving Náto. She loved him with everything in her.

She sent him a letter with a copy of the ultrasound picture and her engagement ring. He was to come put the ring back on her finger if he wanted her. But he never did.

"Then you knew about my mom being pregnant?" Lola asked Esteban agitated.

"No! I didn't know she was pregnant, Lola," he said trying to explain.

"But my Madrina just said …" Lola started to say.

"Míja, we were wrong. Both your mother and I were wrong," said Ana.

Esteban explained his side of the story from the beginning.

He remembered the day he saw Amelia. She was so beautiful. He couldn't take his eyes off of her. She was so alive and vivacious. And she had an amazing personality. It was like she made people want to smile around her.

"Yep. That was my mom," said Lola cracking a smile.

She always thought Esteban was too serious of a name for him. So, she called him by his nickname, Náto. And that's how she introduced him to everyone.

They started spending more time together and getting closer. Before he knew it, he wanted to spend the rest of his life with her and proposed.

The day of the wedding, he was at the airport headed for Miami. Maritza called him saying Mauricio was dying. He thought it was a joke at first. He even got mad at her assuming she was playing games. But a nurse got on the phone and confirmed the story. So, he hauled ass to the hospital.

A few days later, he went to Miami. And that's when his world changed forever.

"So, I still don't understand. If you knew she was pregnant, why didn't you go to her," questioned Lola.

"I received a letter from your mother about two weeks after I got back from Miami. It said she was moving to Europe and returned my ring," said Esteban.

"That's a lie," said Lola.

"I know that now, but I assumed it was true at the time," said Esteban.

"Why?" wondered Lola.

He told her about the restaurant incident.

The day he arrived in Miami, he looked for Amelia. He went by her house, but she wasn't there. However, Ana was and told him where to find her. When he pulled up to the restaurant, he saw her kissing David.

"Padrino! You and mom?" questioned Lola surprised.

"It wasn't like that," said David. "But I'll explain after."

Esteban parked the car and argued with David. Amelia jumped in between them. That's when Esteban turned and snatched the necklace off her neck. He didn't feel she deserved it for trying to protect David and not stand up for him. Amelia just pushed David in the car and they left. Esteban was enraged.

Hours later, Esteban went back to her house. He desperately wanted to fix things. He loved her so much and just wanted to explain what happened. But through her window, he saw her and David again.

David opened a ring box and took the ring out. He slid it on her finger. She stretched her hand out looking at it from afar. Then, she hugged him so excitedly. The logical assumption was he had just proposed. He thought he was too late and went back to New York. And he only married Maritza after finding out she was pregnant with EJ.

David told his story last.

David and Natalie were friends before he ever met Ana. He even had a crush on Natalie, but she was in love with Náto. So, he knew he didn't have a chance.

Then, David met Ana. In a short period of time, she captured his heart. He fell in love with her and knew he wanted to spend the rest of his life with her.

David met Natalie at the restaurant to tell her about Ana. But that's when he found out they were best friends. That threw him for a loop.

The kiss outside was unintentional. Natalie was just feeling depressed and vulnerable from Náto standing her, so she kissed him. Esteban just happened to walk up when she did it. She jumped between them because she wanted to explain that it wasn't David's fault. But couldn't because things got so heated.

Later that night, David went to show Natalie the ring he bought for Ana. Natalie immediately asked to try it on. David didn't mind and slid it on her finger. Then, after looking at it, she hugged him and congratulated him. She was so excited for him and her best friend. And again, Esteban just so happened to see that transpire.

Everyone understood how Esteban made his assumption.

From the outside, anyone would have thought the same thing, even David admitted to how bad it must have looked.

"Why didn't you fight for her? You should've knocked on the door. You should've done something. Why would you let the love of your life go just like that," Lola asked Esteban.

"Sweetheart, I thought about doing that and much more. But it came down to your mother's happiness. I loved her enough to let her go. I thought she chose him and I had to accept that. I couldn't force her to be with me."

"What a mess," said Lola.

Darlene told Lola they started piecing things together the day she had lunch with Esteban and ran into David. That was the same day Ana saw her wearing the necklace.

"So, you thought Amelia married David and left the country this whole time? And never knew she had a kid?" Mauricio asked Esteban.

"That's correct, Míjo."

"And Madrina…You didn't know him by Esteban because mom called him Náto?" questioned Lola.

"That's right, Míja," said Ana.

"And you thought my mom's name was Amelia this whole time?" Lola asked Esteban.

"Yes," he said.

"So, what happened to my mom's ring," asked Lola.

"You're wearing it," said Esteban.

"This was the ring you gave my mom?" she asked even more surprised.

"Yes. It was my mother's."

Lola took the ring off and tried to return it to Esteban.

He wouldn't accept it. So, she set it on the table and asked everyone to leave. She was exhausted and couldn't deal with anything else.

"Lola…" said Ana.

"Madrina, please leave. I'm tired. I'm hurt. I'm confused. And I don't want to hear you right now. My mother lied to me. You lied to me. Just go," said Lola.

"Don't be so hard on your godmother, Lola," said David. "She was only trying to protect you."

"David…Not now. Let's go," said Ana obeying Lola's wishes.

Everyone left except Mauricio.

"Hey," he said sitting next to her.

"Hey."

"I'm sorry about all of this."

"It sucks."

"I'm here for you. You know that, right?"

"I don't want you here, either. It's too hard. Just leave me alone."

"Lola, don't do this. Don't shut me out."

"Mauricio, are you serious? I feel like I've been on the worst roller coaster ride ever," she said crying.

"I understand that. I do, but…"

"You can't possibly understand what I'm going through," she said interrupting him. "You can't possibly understand shit!"

"This isn't just happening to you! What about me?" he said with resentment.

"What do you want from me, Mauricio? What?" screamed Lola.

"I don't want you to shut me out," he said as tears fell down his face.

"Just leave. The wedding is off."

"You're not the only one fucking hurting, Lola!"

Lola didn't respond. She just curled up in a fetal position and cried. Mauricio wanted to help, but she wouldn't let him. So, he left.

Chapter 37
<u>Natalie's Gift</u>

Lola woke up the next morning with a pounding headache. Her makeup was smeared and her hair was all over the place. And she had lost her voice a little from screaming so much the night before.

When she opened her eyes, Crystale and Blair were on the other side of the couch. They rushed right over when they heard what happened.

They got up when they heard Lola get up. Again, she cried as she told them the story.

After, they helped her to her room to take a shower and get cleaned up. They saw a chest with a note sitting on her bed, but Lola just walked right passed it. Crystale started the shower for her while Blair took out some clothes.

They all climbed in Lola's bed and interlocked arms once she got out of the shower.

"I'm really sorryabout everything that's happening, Lo," said Blair.

"Yeah, me too," said Crystale.

Lola just couldn't believe her luck.

"Well, Mauricio's not doing well either," said Crystale.

"I'm sure he's not. And I know I was mean to him. But how do I deal with this? I'm in love with my brother. Who does this honestly happen to?" asked Lola.

"I overheard Mauricio telling Wyatt he's leaving for LA tonight. He can't deal with everything going on. He'll be back for the wedding though," said Crystale.

Lola didn't say anything. She just cried.

"I just don't want to think about it anymore. I want it all to go away," said Lola. "I'm so heartbroken."

They just comforted their friend.

"Are you hungry?" Crystale asked Lola.

"No."

"So, what's in the chest?" Blair asked Lola pointing to it.

"I don't know."

"Do you feel like opening it?" asked Crystale.

"Ok," said Lola shrugging her shoulders.

Lola reached for the card. It was from Ana. She read it out loud.

"Mija, I love you. And I hope this helps you understand some things better. Love, your Madrina".

Lola opened the chest. The first thing she saw was an envelope that said "Read first". She removed the envelope and glanced at what was inside. There were all kinds of trinkets, memorabilia, pictures, videos and letters inside. A picture of her mother with Esteban caught her eye. Then, she picked up a little photo album. Inside were menus or receipts from restaurants they had gone to, dead flowers from their dates and little things from hotels where they stayed. Lola put everything down and opened the envelope. It was a letter from her mother. Lola started crying. She knew she wouldn't be able to read it. So, Crystale read it while Blair held her in his arms.

The letter told Lola many truths. The first was the truth about her father. His real name, where he lived and other stuff that coincided with what everyone told her last night.

She told her different things about her and Esteban. And the reason why she didn't want her to know the truth about him.

Natalie didn't want Lola to ever have to deal with Maritza. She knew Maritza wasn't a good person. And Natalie gave her some examples to back up her reasoning. So, she made it clear that she made the choice to separate them, not anyone else.

Next, Natalie told her she had a brother and his name was Mauricio.

Then, she explained some of the other things in the chest. For example, Lola's real birth certificate with her father's name on it, her journals, articles and a picture of her paternal grandmother, whom she looked exactly like.

Last, Natalie told her not to be mad at Ana. She made Ana promise to never tell a soul. Not even David unless it was absolutely necessary. So, if she was reading the letter, it became just that…Necessary!!!

She admitted to making lots of mistakes, but Lola wasn't one of them. And she would go through any length to protect her like she did. She ended the letter with an apology about lying to her about her father and words of encouragement.

It was a relief hearing her mother's words. But she wanted to be left alone while she went through the chest in its entirety. Blair and Crystale didn't really want to leave her alone, but did. They made her promise to call if she needed anything.

Lola sat on the floor and spread everything out. She sat there going through every little detail. She found her ultrasound picture, locks of her hair and a few of her teeth that had fallen out. There were lots of pictures of her and Esteban. And there were more revealing items in there.

She popped in a video and sat there crying while watching her mom. She missed her so much and needed her at that very moment.

Lola felt a little better afterwards. She even cracked a smile looking at everything on the floor. It was good seeing her mom.

She called her godparents over so they could talk. They were there in ten minutes.

She forgave them and just talked to them about everything that happened. They told her everything they knew and answered all of her questions honestly.

Then, Lola asked David if she could talk to Ana alone. He went home while they went upstairs to her room. She wanted to show her everything that was in the chest and talk about her mother. Ana knew her mother better than anyone in the world. And Lola made Ana watch a few videos with her.

Before leaving, Ana made her some food. She knew Lola hadn't eaten and wanted to make sure she did.

Lola served herself a big plate of spaghetti and sat on the couch to watch her birthday videos. She laughed and cried. She missed Mauricio more than anyone knew. They were together everyday, except when he traveled for business. And she wasn't used to not talking to him.

Then, she got an overwhelming feeling to throw up and ran to the bathroom. She couldn't imagine being pregnant on top of everything else.

She ran out and bought a pregnancy test. Her results came back negative.

Chapter 38
<u>Crystale's Wedding</u>

The day had finally come for Crystale to get married. And the weather couldn't have been more perfect.

Crystale's dream wedding venue was the Biltmore Hotel in Coral Gables. This historic, but legendary resort accommodated all of Crystale's wedding needs. From the Al Capone suite to the courtyard ceremony and grand ballroom reception. She had it all. Not to mention picturesque garden backgrounds for captivating photos.

Crystale loved purple. It was her favorite color. So, it was incorporated with black and white to create an elegant and romantic courtyard ceremony.

The courtyard looked amazing. Purple and white candles illuminated the entire area. Purple uplighting added that touch of color she wanted. Huge purple, white and black floral arrangements were everywhere. White chiavari chairs with black cushions and purple chiffon sashes filled the courtyard. A purple and black aisle runner created the pathway. The fountain water had purple lighting. Tall lighted trees and plush gardens added beauty. Custom-made lanterns draped the guests' seating area. The altar was an enormous garden arbor with intricate metal detailing accompanied with Roman columns, a gazillion flowers, lots of fabrics and candles.

As the wedding party lined up, Mauricio and Lola saw each other for the first time in almost a month. They just stared at each other and smiled. It was obvious their hearts couldn't grasp being siblings. She loved this man and missed him desperately. And Mauricio looked the same way.

All the groomsmen and best man wore black Calvin Klein tuxedos with purple ties and purple boutonnieres. They were all freshly groomed, manicured and smelling good.

Wyatt wore all black. His black Calvin Klein tux was worn with a black tie and a white boutonniere. And his accessories were simple: a Cartier watch.

The bridesmaids wore two-piece, A-line, floor length dresses with a halter neckline. The tops were purple satin with a black satin skirt. A black lace band wrapped around their torsos with a purple ribbon around the lace. The matron of honor wore a black lace, scalloped halter top with a side bow and a white, long, satin skirt.

Their hair was swept to one side with diamond pins in it. They wore diamond droplet necklace sets with matching earrings and bracelets. Their bouquets were made of black and purple mini calla lilies.

The ceremony began promptly at 6:00 p.m. Music played as each couple made their way down the aisle.

Then, the purple part of the aisle runner was lifted leaving a black runner for Crystale to walk down. Her two hundred guests stood to their feet when '*Because you loved me*' by Celine Dion played.

Crystale slowly appeared on her father's arm. Wyatt's eyes watered. She looked so beautiful.

She wore a custom made Badgley and Mischka wedding

dress. It was a fitting A-line, halter dress with a half back. The bodice was satin and covered in crystal beading. The skirt was a ruffled organza taffeta that cascaded down into a chapel train. Her hair was down in cascading curls with a Swarovski crystal double headband. She wore a more extravagant diamond droplet necklace set with earrings and bracelets to match. And her bouquet was made of black, white and purple calla lilies with Cymbidium orchids and crystal pins all over.

The ceremony lasted just under thirty minutes. They exchanged their own vows and Cartier wedding bands.

The guests were escorted to the second floor patio area for the cocktail hour while the bridal party took their pictures. Crystale and Wyatt included a white 1964 Rolls Royce Cloud III in their photos. Lola and Mauricio also took pictures together.

The reception was a grand event as well. It took place in the Granada Ballroom. High ceilings with hand painted art, Roman styled architecture and expensive crystal chandeliers embellished the room. Purple pinched satin tablecloths with black satin chair covers and purple satin sashes dressed the furniture. Huge purple, black and white floral arrangements sat high as centerpieces. Candles, menu cards and favors sat on the tables. Purple lighting illuminated the room. And their four-tiered cake by Devine Delicacies stood out as a focal point. The cake was white with purple satin bows. Rhinestone initials topped it off.

Lola felt a mild pain in her stomach as they waited for the bride and groom to enter the room for their first dance. It didn't last long though. So, she didn't worry about it.

All the guests stood to their feet to clap and cheer as the newlyweds were announced. They immediately went to the smoke-filled dance floor. They danced to Michael Bolton's *'When a man loves a woman'*. This was Wyatt's favorite song. And he dedicated it to Crystale.

After their dance, Crystale changed into her second dress made by Monique Lhuillier. It was a fitting white satin, floor length, halter dress with a sweep train. The deep V neckline met at the wide band of crystal beading wrapped around her upper torso. It was the only bling on the dress. It was simple, but elegant.

Mauricio and Carla made their best man and matron of honor speeches as dinner was being served. Lola, Blair, Robert and their parents also said a few words.

Then, Lola, Blair, Mauricio and Ivan made an announcement.

"Hi, Everyone. We have a special announcement to make," said Lola over the microphone.

"Mr. And Mrs. Whitfield…We have a special surprise for you," said Blair.

"We are gifting you the best honeymoon ever," said Mauricio.

"We hope you like it," said Ivan.

A waiter handed the newlyweds an envelope.

"For your honeymoon, we got you a ten-day trip to Greece. The first two nights you'll stay at the Hotel Grande Breta in Athens. You'll enjoy gourmet cuisine, 24-hour hotel amenities and experience Greek culture," said Lola passing the microphone.

"Then, you'll spend the next four days at Hotel Cavol

Tagool in Mykonos. You'll enjoy luxury, comfort and style while indulging in the endless blue ocean," said Mauricio.

"And you'll spend the last four days at Androni's Luxury Resort in Sanorini. You'll bask in relaxation while enjoying the hillside city view," said Ivan.

"This all-expense paid trip is filled with lots of romantic surprises. So, relax, enjoy and oh…Don't come back pregnant," said Blair making a joke.

Everyone laughed because they knew she already was.

"Congratulations!!!!" they all said together.

Everyone clapped and cheered. Crystale and Wyatt got up and hugged them all. They were very surprised and very grateful.

As the party got started, Lola's pains grew progressively worse. Mauricio saw her in a corner balled up and went to her.

"Baby Girl, you okay?" he asked.

"No. My stomach hurts really bad," she said hunched over.

He picked her up discreetly and took her outside the ballroom. He quietly went and got Ana. She asked him to take them to the hospital. From the sound of it, Lola was losing her baby.

Chapter 39
Lola at the Hospital

They made it to the hospital in ten minutes. As soon as Mauricio picked her up to take her inside, blood started dripping down her leg. He got really scared. When the hospital staff saw them, they immediately rushed to help.

The nurse kept asking him a bunch of questions, but he couldn't answer any of them. Mauricio was still in shock from what Ana said. So, Ana stepped in and gave them Lola's history.

Ana called everyone while with the nurses to tell them where she was. But they were to be as discreet as possible. It was Crystale's wedding day and she should finish her evening.

Ana went to Mauricio who was going crazy just crying. She told him what was happening to Lola. She hugged him tight as they fell to the floor. She just stayed there with him, holding him.

"What happened? Why didn't I know she was pregnant? Did she stop loving me?" were questions that came out of his mouth.

"No, Mauricio. Lola still loves you. She loves you more than life itself. She just found out last week and was going to tell you tonight," said Ana rubbing his head.

She explained how Lola took a pregnancy test the night after the truth came out, but the results were negative. She even had her period. But last week, she went to the doctor 'cause she wasn't feeling well. The doctor confirmed that she was around four weeks pregnant.

"Why is this happening to her? Why is she losing my baby?" he asked.

Ana talked about the high levels of stress she'd been under and how life's been for her since everything happened. It was too much at one time. Her body just couldn't handle it anymore is what she figured.

Then, David, Esteban, Darlene, Blair, Ivan and EJ showed up and found them on the floor. David was about to rush them, when she put her hand out. Blair just covered his mouth and started crying. It was such a sad scene.

"Míjo," said Esteban reaching for him. "Míjo, come here."

"Bruh, you alright. Ricio...Come on man," said EJ picking him up crying with him.

David and Esteban helped EJ with Mauricio. Blair and Ivan stood with Ana. There wasn't a dry eye in the place.

An hour later, the doctor came out and advised everyone that she was fine. She had in fact miscarried.

"Can she have more kids?" asked Mauricio.

"Yes, she can," said the doctor.

Then, Crystale, Wyatt, Carla, Bynum, Robert, Janelle, Janelle's daughter, Crystale's parents and Blair's family came running through the door. Wyatt's parents stayed to attend to their remaining guests.

"Why the hell didn't anyone tell me about Lola?" yelled Crystale upset.

"It's your wedding day, Crissy and we didn't want to…" Blair started to say.

"Don't give me that shit, Blair! It's Lola! It's always been us three. And it'll always be that way!" she said crying. "Don't you ever do that to me again!"

Blair apologized and hugged her. He told her to calm down because of the baby. Wyatt and Robert saw Mauricio and went to him.

Ana told everyone what happened and why she lost the baby. Crystale cried even harder and wondered why Lola never said anything. Ana told them she wanted to talk to Mauricio first.

The nurse came out and said three people could see her at a time. There was no question who the first three were. Mauricio, Crystale and Blair sprinted off.

When they walked in, she was still groggy from the anesthesia.

"Hey, Baby Girl," said Mauricio rubbing her hair.

"Hey, Lo," said Blair and Crystale.

She looked around with her eyes half open.

Mauricio got in her face and said, "I love you, Baby Girl. And I don't care what our blood says. You're my woman. And you should've told me I was gonna be a dad. I would've been here sooner."

"I'm sorry," she whispered as tears began to fall down the side of her face.

"Shhhh...Don't talk, Lo," said Blair crying and all emotional from what Mauricio had just said.

"And we're gonna fight when you get outta here," said Crystale smiling, but crying.

Lola cracked a smile as more tears fell. They hugged her trying to comfort her.

Esteban peeked his head in and asked to speak to Mauricio. He quickly kissed Lola on the forehead and told her he loved her.

Esteban, Mauricio and EJ went down the hall to one of the empty hospital rooms.

"This may not be the best time, but I need to speak to you both," said Esteban.

First, he told EJ about Lola being his sister and explained the short version of the story. EJ was pleasantly surprised, but upset that no one said anything before now. He thought Mauricio had just gone off on business. Esteban apologized, but asked that nothing be said until he was certain of something else first. When EJ inquired what that something was, Esteban didn't say a word. He turned to Mauricio and handed him an envelope.

"What's this, Papí?" he asked.

"Just open it," Esteban said turning away, crying.

EJ hugged his dad as Mauricio opened the letter.

"Papí, what's wrong?" asked EJ wondering why his father was breaking down.

"Papí, what's this? What does this mean?" asked Mauricio.

It was DNA results for Mauricio's paternity test. Esteban wasn't his real father. But, Esteban quickly assured him that he was his son no matter what any results said. He loved him like his own and always would. Mauricio and EJ were his pride and joy.

But, they continued to just ask more questions.

Esteban explained his suspicions regarding their paternity. He had them both tested. EJ was his biological child. Mauricio wasn't.

"All this time I thought he wasn't your son. But it turns out I'm the real bastard," said Mauricio angrily hitting the table hard, crying his eyes out.

Esteban grabbed him. "Mauricio, look at me. Look at me!" said Esteban in a stern and semi-loud voice. "Don't you EVER think you're not my son! Do you hear me? I raised you! I took care of you! I instilled my values and integrity in you! You're my heir! And no one…I mean NO ONE can take that from us! Do you hear me?"

Mauricio nodded and cried on his father's shoulder as he hugged him tight.

"Ricio…Bruh…I'm here for you, Man. I love you and I'll always be your brother," said EJ joining in on the hug.

Esteban told him he would've never had him tested because he was his son regardless. But, he couldn't take seeing him and Lola suffer anymore. It was too painful watching them and he felt compelled to do something. He knew if there was a chance he could fix things, he had to try. But, he admitted that he feared rejection if either one wasn't his son.

Mauricio now turned to Esteban and reassured him that that would never happen. He wasn't going anywhere. Esteban was the only man he knew and wanted to know as his father. Mauricio thanked him for being there and never leaving even when he could have. He was the man he was today because of Esteban. And he wanted them to be even closer if that was possible. That made Esteban happy and relieved.

"I love you, Papí," said Mauricio squeezing him tight.

"I love you too, Míjo," said Esteban squeezing him back. "So very much," he said crying.

Esteban reached in his pocket and gave Mauricio Lola's engagement ring back.

"You might need this again now that you know the truth," Esteban told Mauricio.

"Where did you get it from, Papí?"

"Ana. The nurse gave it to her when Lola was admitted. She was wearing it on a necklace."

Mauricio thanked him and took off down the hall to Lola's room. By this time, she was more awake.

"Marry me," said Mauricio busting through the door.

Lola just gave him a look.

"Do you love me?" he asked her.

"Yes."

"Then, marry me. Just say yes," he said sliding her ring back on her finger.

"Mauricio…"

He told her what Esteban just told him.

Chapter 40
Esteban's day in Court

It was Mauricio's birthday, but it was also his parents' final divorce hearing. Mauricio and Lola flew to New York to be with Esteban. They knew how hard it would be for him and didn't want to leave him alone. EJ also went to support his father.

It had been a real war between the couple and their attorneys. Maritza was determined to take everything Esteban had. But, he had other plans.

Maritza testified in court first. She attempted to prove Esteban's worth by providing his accounting firm's bank statements and company records. It was to justify her desired spousal support. She also advised the court of his earned profits from investments. She felt he should maintain the lifestyle she was accustomed to living.

Esteban, in turn, provided the court with current company records. The company hadn't made the kind of money she was insinuating. It actually lost money. She provided the court with records from two years ago. And with regards to his investments, it hadn't produced much recently because of the downturn in the economy. The profits earned that she spoke about occurred almost two years ago as well and were spent on remodeling their home, a new car for her and multiple shopping sprees she went on. He'd also donated to his favorite charities. He provided receipts for everything. So, he wasn't worth what she claimed.

Then, Esteban testified, sharing all the stuff she'd been hiding. She had an investment portfolio that was worth a little something. But she jumped in and explained it was worth minimal. She had made bad investments and lost the money. She just so happen to have the current statement to prove her accusations.

Next, Esteban provided evidence of her purchasing two homes in the Dominican Republic with his money and without his knowledge. Again, she jumped in. She admitted she bought them. However, one of them was for her mother and the other was a vacation home for the family. He thought she might say that. So, his attorney demonstrated that she'd purchased the vacation home to generate income. And she hadn't contributed one dime of it to the family.

His attorney also revealed that she'd been hiding money in three offshore accounts. She tried denying it, but he had proof of that as well.

Esteban told the court about her secret stash of jewelry in a bank safe deposit box. He provided photos of all the pieces and the registration card of the box. She explained that he bought them for her and wanted to keep it in a safe place. But Esteban denied buying any of it. He showed the court where, how and when she purchased that jewelry.

Then, he got dirty. His attorney provided evidence of her infidelity throughout their marriage. She denied everything, but couldn't after his surprises.

Esteban's attorney summoned five of the many men she'd slept with. She paid them, bought them things and traveled with Esteban's money. They all told the court how she bragged about using him and his money. She even purchased a brownstone in Brooklyn for one of them. Esteban's attorney provided the evidence on how she purchased it. He also provided statements of her spending habits with these men.

And to drive it home, Esteban shared Mauricio's DNA results with the court. He took care of a child that wasn't biologically his for almost thirty years. And she knew it. He showed the court Mauricio's original birth certificate registered in the Dominican Republic and told the court how and why suspicions were raised. She had nothing to say.

Each attorney gave closing statements and reiterated how they wanted the assets split.

Esteban wanted his divorce finalized with no spousal support awarded. He wanted to sell their Park Avenue home and keep the proceeds. The vacation home and her mother's home in D.R. should be awarded to him. She should sell her investment portfolio and split the profits since the initial money came from him. He wanted to keep her secret jewelry stash. And the money in the three off-shore accounts should be returned to him. She could keep her car. All accounts and debt they had together should be dissolved and separated. And she should pay him the current market price of $2 million for the brownstone in Brooklyn or it be turned over to him.

Maritza disagreed. She wanted the divorce with her maiden name restored, spousal support of $25,000 per month and the Park Avenue penthouse with all monthly expenses paid. The vacation home in D.R. should be

awarded to her. Her mother should keep her home in
D.R. Since there wasn't much left, she agreed to sell her
investment portfolio and split the proceeds. She wanted
to keep her jewelry. The three accounts should be divided
as follows: the smallest account to EJ, the second smallest
account to Mauricio and she keep the largest account for
herself. She wanted to retain all of her personal belongings
and gifts that she acquired over the years in the marriage.
And she wanted Esteban was to pay her legal fees.

After deliberating, the judge came back with some harsh
words for Maritza. He told her that she had no scruples and
what she had done to Esteban was an injustice. The judge
went on to tell her that he had been a good provider, father
and husband. He did everything he was supposed to do for
his family.

The judge then ruled in favor of Esteban. The following
was effective immediately:

The divorce was granted and her maiden name was
restored. No spousal support was awarded. The Park
Avenue penthouse was to be sold and the proceeds split
50-50 between Maritza and Esteban. The vacation home in
the Dominican Republic was to be sold. Esteban, Maritza,
Mauricio and EJ would each receive 25% of the proceeds
since she mentioned it was for the family. Her mother's
home was paid for by Esteban. So, she had five days to
return the purchasing price of the home or it would be
retained by Esteban. Her investment portfolio was to be
sold and split 50-50 between her and Esteban. Maritza's
three off-shore accounts would be split as follows: EJ
was awarded the smallest amount of $401,500; Mauricio

received the second smallest amount of $995,500; and Esteban received the largest amount of $2.5M. Esteban was awarded the secret jewelry stash, since he pretty much bought it all. She was able to keep her personal belongings, gifted items during the marriage and her car. The judge ordered all accounts and debt be dissolved and separated. The cash in their current bank account was to be split 50-50. She was responsible for paying her own legal fees. And the judge ordered the purchase price of the brownstone in Brooklyn, which was $1.2 million, be returned within fourteen days or the brownstone would be turned over to Esteban as well.

Esteban was elated. Justice had finally been served. His kids hugged and congratulated him with excitement. However, Maritza was pissed and stormed off.

Esteban went back to his attorney's office to do all the necessary paperwork and cancel frozen accounts. Lola texted Darlene to go ahead with the plans Esteban had in place. Maritza's attorney immediately placed a lien on her assets until full payment was received.

Meanwhile, Lola took Mauricio out to lunch for his birthday. They went to his favorite restaurant and then went shopping. She bought him lots of stuff and gave him the watch she'd bought in Turks and Caicos.

That evening, Lola and Mauricio went to the Park Avenue home. It was time to face the music. Mauricio wanted to talk with his mom and clear the air.

Esteban had other plans. He went home to his new place where Darlene was waiting for him.

"Hi," he said walking through the door.

"Well, hello...Mr. Free Man," she said with her arms extended out for a hug and a kiss.

Esteban was the official owner of a mansion on the Upper East Side of Manhattan. It had five floors, two basements and an additional garden level. There were soaring ceilings, a spectacular marble staircase and grand-scaled rooms. This New York palace sat on East 70th Street between 5th and Madison.

She took him on a tour of the main level, which was fully furnished. It was the only level Darlene had had time to decorate.

She went to a desk, took out an envelope and handed it to Esteban. It was the deed to his new place. That's what Lola's text was about. The plan was for Darlene to make the final payment and have the property transferred into his name as soon as she received a text from Lola. He finally had a home to call his own.

They went upstairs to the third floor where his bedroom was. There were candles lit everywhere and champagne chilling. She went to change into something a little more comfortable. When she came out, he was tongue tied.

"You look so beautiful," he told her.

"Thank you."

She drew near him and kissed him.

"I've waited so long for this," he said.

"Me, too."

They got busy right then and there. They didn't get to the champagne. Esteban was more interested in making love to Darlene. He enjoyed every minute of it.

Chapter 41
Maritza returns home

The next morning, Maritza returned home mean, bitter and way too tipsy. She was rude to all of the contractors and designers she saw there.

"What the hell is goin' here?" she yelled slightly slurring.

"Maritza! Lower your voice," said Esteban.

"I don't have to listen to you, anymore!"

"You're so embarrassing."

"I don't care."

Esteban explained that he was remodeling the penthouse to increase its value. He wanted to get as much money out of it as he could. She didn't argue there.

Then, she looked by the staircase and saw four suitcases.

"Why are my bags out here?" she questioned.

Everyone had to leave the house for a week while construction was taking place. So, two of the suitcases were hers and two were his.

He took the liberty of arranging for her to go to the Dominican Republic to stay with her mother. He was also sending a realtor down there to check out the properties. He wanted to sell the vacation home as soon as possible. And her mother's house would be checked out too. However, she didn't want him anywhere near her mother's house. But, he didn't care seeing that it might be his. She assured him he would have his money in three days.

Then, she saw Lola speaking to the designers and contractors.

"What the hell do you think you're doing?!?" Maritza yelled at Lola from across the room.

"Ma!" said Mauricio. "Don't talk to her that way. And we need to talk."

"I have nothin' to say to you. And she better get the hell out of this house."

"She's not going anywhere!" exclaimed Esteban. "So shut your mouth!"

"And we do have stuff to talk about," said Mauricio. "For starters, why did you lie to me about my real father?"

"You don't want to know the truth. You can't handle the truth!" exclaimed Maritza mocking the quote.

"He deserves to know, Maritza," said Esteban.

"You want the truth…"

Mauricio was her love child with her high school sweetheart and true love, Carlos. They dated until she left the Dominican Republic to come to New York. Even after moving, she would go back home to see him all the time.

However, she saw opportunity in Esteban. He was working at his father's accounting firm at the time, which was starting to take off. And since she didn't want to work, she figured she could live off him and support Carlos at the same time.

She used Esteban's money to attain hers and Carlos' three businesses in D.R., a hotel and two restaurants. She also bought their dream home, which she said was her mother's.

The downer for her was EJ. She didn't want another

kid, especially by Esteban. But he was her ticket to living lavishly and having Carlos, who was also about that money.

She went on to talk about how she wouldn't have had anything if she hadn't given Mauricio those pills that almost killed him the day Esteban was leaving for Miami. She knew she had to do something drastic to stop him.

"How could you do that to your own son? He almost died!" yelled Esteban.

"I didn't care! I wasn't gonna let you marry your sweet Amelia! I put in three years. And she comes along and like that," said Maritza snapping her fingers, "You wanted to marry her. Hell no!"

Tears fell from Mauricio's eyes. He couldn't believe what he was hearing. And Lola was steaming.

"Maybe she was a better person than you!" yelled Lola.

"And she loved me!" yelled Esteban.

Maritza's anger turned to laughter as she laughed at them both. "Yeah…I know. She sounded so pathetic in her letter. She talked about loving you and wanting you, her and the baby to be a family," said Maritza carrying on as if it were a joke.

"So, YOU took that letter?" guessed Esteban.

"Duh…" she said laughing.

"And you knew I had another child out there this whole time?" asked Esteban.

"Yep. I knew. But did you honestly think I would give you that letter and ultrasound picture? I'm not that stupid," said Maritza as she kept laughing. "You would've left me. So, I typed one up saying she was moving. I needed to throw you off and make you forget about her."

Maritza walked over to a painting that hung on the living room wall. She took it down, untapped an envelope from the back and threw it at him. It was the letter and the picture.

"You're a FUCKIN' MONSTER!" Esteban shouted in disbelief.

"Well, not quite. But that is why I got pregnant. I needed a legitimate child of yours, too. That way, you would always have to support me if you didn't marry me."

"You're the devil herself!" said Esteban boiling hot.

"Thank you, but I see it as being the type of girl to get what she wants. And right now I want to go to D.R., see my man, fuck him in our bed and lay up in our house that's paid for. I'll be back in a week for my money," she said.

"You're a fuckin' BITCH!" yelled Lola.

"I know," she said with a smile.

As she approached the front door, she said, "Oh...Would you like to meet your father, Mauricio?"

Mauricio just shook his head in amazement.

"Suit yourself," she said shrugging her shoulders as she grabbed her luggage.

Maritza didn't even make it to the door before Lola slapped the shit out of her. She just couldn't take it anymore. Maritza tried to slap her back, but never got the chance. Lola slapped her a couple of more times. Mauricio had to restrain her.

"You'll pay for that, you little Whore!" said Maritza.

"And you'll rot in hell, Bitch!" screamed Lola.

Chapter 42
The Bahamas

Lola and Mauricio were scheduled to catch a noon flight to the Bahamas for Mauricio's birthday surprise. But after Maritza's malicious ranting of the truth, they delayed their departure by a couple of hours. The shock hadn't worn off and they still had to finish helping with the contractors and designers.

Lola reserved a three-day trip at a new resort on a private island just off the coast of Nassau called Sunset Horizons. It was an exclusive and all-inclusive adult resort that catered to couples. This was the place to rejuvenate a relationship and turn up the romance. And with only thirty 2-bedroom private bungalows, it was a true getaway.

They flew into Nassau. Then took a ferry to their paradise island.

As the ferry circled the island, tall jungle-like trees surrounded each bungalow for privacy. There were private pools, outdoor showers and large outdoor decks as part of the outdoor amenties. All of the bungalows had walls of windows, allowing them to catch a glimpse of the luxurious indoor, theme-styled living spaces. And they also had access to their very own private beach, chef and maid.

Lola and Mauricio had an Asian-themed bungalow with lots of radiant colors. It went nicely with the natural wood furnishings and flooring. There was a fully stocked bar and plenty of adult entertainment. But the best part was the ocean view through the huge glass windows. It was breathtaking. The brochures didn't do it justice.

"This is very nice," said Mauricio. "Thank you, Baby."

She tipped the resort attendant as he left.

"You're welcome and Happy Birthday, Baby," said Lola giving him a kiss.

"Thank you."

Lola pulled him into the bathroom where a trail of red rose petals and candles led to a tub filled with lots of bubbles. She wanted to romance her man as soon as they got there.

As they sat in the tub, they talked and just enjoyed each other's company.

Then, Mauricio brought up the topic of sex.

"Baby Girl, do you think you're ready?" he asked.

"I've been ready, Baby, " she said touching his face.

"'Cause I'm not sure I can hold back once I get all that lovin'. You know how I like it."

Lola laughed and said, "I know, Baby. And there are no restrictions. Our six weeks have been passed."

She kissed him and started massaging him. He instantly got hard. They got out and went to the bedroom. They kissed passionately as he picked her up and laid her on the bed. He couldn't wait to be inside of her.

He slowly slid inside her. As he pushed deeper, she let out one helluva scream. Mauricio got scared and pulled out.

"Baby, I'm sorry. Did I hurt you?" he asked fearful that she wasn't completely healed.

"I'm fine. Just fuck me!" she yelled breathing heavily.

So, he did. He slowly went deep inside of her. She

grabbed him so tight that her nails dug into his back. But he didn't care. She felt so good. Her savored every stroke. And it was more erotic in front of the big, open window overlooking the ocean. They took their time and made sweet, passionate love.

After a couple of hours, they finished round one. She had a surprise planned for him, so they needed to leave the bungalow.

"Babe, let's go to the beach," she said changing into her tiny bikini.

"Ok," he said laying there relaxing with his eyes closed.

"Here, I brought your swimming trunks," she said throwing them at him.

He lay there for a few more minutes. When he finally sat up and saw Lola, he couldn't believe what she had on.

"Damn, Baby!!! Come here," he said.

Her string bikini only covered the essentials. The top had two strips of material covering her nipples and the bottoms had one narrow piece of material covering her front. Her backside was hanging all out.

"You're sexy as HELL, Baby Girl!" he yelled.

"Thank you, Baby," she said kissing him. "But let's go."

He finally got up so they could go swimming.

They spent about an hour at the beach before heading to the resort's bar. She needed to distract him a little longer. So, they went to enjoy a few drinks and play a game of pool. Along the way, they picked up some souvenirs from the local boutiques and shops.

In the middle of their second game of billiards, she got a phone call. It was time to go.

As they approached their bungalow, lights beamed from the glass windows. As they got closer, there were candles everywhere. It was so romantic in the middle of a tropical paradise.

Their chef was preparing a four-course meal when they walked in. So, they quickly showered and changed.

They only got through the conch fritters and fresh conch salad when Mauricio excused the chef. He tipped him and asked him to return later. He wanted to feel Lola's insides again so bad.

After three hours of pleasuring one another, Mauricio called the chef back. They had worked up quite an appetite.

They spent the rest of their time there making love over and over again.

Chapter 43
Darlene in Dominican Republic

Esteban sent Darlene to the Dominican Republic the same day Mauricio and Lola left to the Bahamas. She was only gonna be there a few hours. Esteban was anxious to tie up all loose ends with Maritza.

He rented Darlene a jet, arranged ground transportation and transportation between cities. The vacation home in Punta Cana was her first stop. After, she was going to the house in Cabarete.

When Darlene landed in Punta Cana, she was greeted by two men that Esteban contracted to inspect the property. They drove to the home where Maritza's agent was there waiting with an engineer to do the same.

This vacation home was nothing short of a luxurious mansion estate in the upscale and pristine resort of Tortuga Bay. The two-story, five-bedroom/six-bath home sat nestled between coral reefs and rocky cliffs. The exterior was made of stone and stucco with a red brick round driveway, manicured landscaping and a water fountain with a pond.

Inside was just as nice with dark wood beams that ran across the high vaulted ceilings. The windows and doors had the same dark wood shutters. Coral stoned walls and floors complimented the stucco hallways. The living room and dining room were very spacious with ocean and mountainous views. It had an Italian modular kitchen with natural granite countertops. There were two pools and a heated Jacuzzi with an outside bar and three Tiki huts. The rear had two guest quarters with a maid's quarter.

Darlene took lots of pictures and videos. She uploaded them to her laptop to show a potential client. And she was certain she had a deal contingent upon the selling price.

After the inspection, the men appraised the house at $975K. There was some major damage and neglect issues that Maritza never tended to. So, the cost of fixing everything had to be deducted from its real value.

Mario, Maritza's agent, called Maritza. She wasn't gonna be happy with their findings and estimated worth. But, she had no one to blame but herself.

Darlene called her client. He offered $700K. Maritza didn't agree. So, Darlene called Esteban to inform him of everything. He then called Maritza. He was in agreement if it meant selling right away. But she wasn't. She wanted more money. But, he threatened to take her back to court regarding Carlos and everything she blabbed about before leaving. So, she had no choice after that.

Thirty minutes later, Darlene's helicopter landed at the house in Cabarete. It landed directly on the property since there was a helipad on the premises.

As a woman approached, Darlene could only assume it was Maritza.

"Hi, I'm Darlene," she said shaking this woman's hand.

"Hi, I'm Maritza."

They got the first order of business out of the way. Maritza signed the contract on the vacation home in Punta Cana.

Then, Maritza gave her a tour of the home. Darlene was

very impressed with Maritza. She'd invested Esteban's money well.

Darlene recorded and took footage of everything.

This multi-leveled mansion sat on four acres of land in a private, gated community. Stunning tropical gardens, manicured landscaping with lots of lighting and unique water statues adorned the exterior.

But the inside…was unbelievable! It had it all…eight bedrooms, ten and half baths, 50-foot ceilings, an open floor plan, grand arches, giant columns and stone flooring. There was a movie theater for twenty, a hydraulic elevator, a pond in the floor of the house and two kitchens.

The kitchen in the main house had stone flooring, Mahogany wood cabinets and stainless steel appliances. The summer kitchen connected to the outside and overlooked the oversized swimming pool area. This natural, tropical kitchen had tile flooring with two refrigerators, ice makers and freezers. There was also a nook area with lots of seating, fire tables and a giant television.

As Darlene walked out further, she saw a massive bar and grilling area, cabanas, more fire tables, a spa pavilion with a massage table, a juice bar, several diving platforms and sunbathing decks.

But, the best part about the pool area was the sunken room. A private room was housed under the pool. It had gaming tables, two saunas, a bar and windows to see into the pool.

And to top it off, there was a fresh water lagoon with white sandy beaches, a basketball court, beach volleyball court, a marina and a lighted pier over the lagoon in the back.

The seven-car garage had three jet skis, a canoe, water tubes, skis, boat equipment, scooters, her Jaguar and a SUV. Her staff included a chef, three maids, three gardeners and two drivers.

Darlene arrived back to New York that same evening and went straight to her office where Esteban awaited. She showed him the signed contract and footage of the mansion in Cabarete.

"This is very nice," said Esteban surprised.

"You should see it in person."

"Oh I will," he said. "And soon."

Darlene did what was asked regarding the contract for the Punta Cana home.

Next, Esteban called Maritza from Darlene's office to tell her about the offers she received on the Park Avenue penthouse. He told her how Darlene showed the unit to a few of New York's finest and they were all interested.

Darlene faxed Maritza six of the ten contracts for her and Esteban to discuss. But it was a no-brainer for Maritza. She accepted the highest offer, which was $20M. Esteban suggested she sign two more just in case the first choice fell through. She faxed them back signed.

Chapter 44
Esteban's Revenge

Maritza returned to New York after a week. She was anxious to get her money and be done with Esteban for good.

She drove up to her building and attempted to enter, but was prohibited. When she started making a scene, Esteban came out followed by two police officers. He signaled for the officers to keep a distance while he spoke to her alone. He was about to unleash his wrath on her.

"What the hell's going on, Esteban?" she asked. "The doorman won't let me in."

"That's because you don't live here anymore," he said.

"What the hell are you talkin' about?"

Immediate occupancy was one of the conditions when the property sold. The new owners were eager to occupy their unit. She had twenty four hours to contest the contract after signing, if she didn't agree or changed her mind. Since she didn't, the sale proceeded. So, she was no longer welcomed there. Also, a restraining order was issued against her in case she caused any problems. She was not to be within 300 feet of the building or new occupants.

"I don't give a shit who bought it. I just want my money and my stuff," she said.

He pulled out a document from the envelope he was holding. It was a statement for ten dollars. The actual check went to her attorney for her legal fees.

"What the fuck is this?" she asked sarcastically.

"This is your half from selling the penthouse," he said smiling.

"BULLSHIT! You're missing a whole lot of zeros. I want my money, Esteban…NOW!" she demanded.

He pulled out a copy of the contract and told her to look closely. What she thought said twenty million really said twenty dollars. In the description, it read "Twenty & million 00/cents", not "Twenty million & 00/cents". She hadn't paid close attention to the "&" sign. Also, what she thought were commas in the number value were actually decimal points. So it read, "20.00.000.000", instead of "$20,000,000.00". It equaled twenty dollars, regardless of the number of zeros.

"You FUCKIN' BASTARD!!!" she yelled.

Then, he handed her two more statements. One for $10 and another for $105. The actual checks also went to her attorney.

As per the divorce settlement, Maritza was awarded half the amount in their joint bank account. The ten dollar statement reflected her half. Esteban cleared their account to pay his attorney and other household expenses first, leaving twenty dollars.

The statement for $105 was from her investment portfolio. It sold for $210 and Esteban took his half, as awarded by the court. Her attorney received the other half.

"And with regards to your stuff…" he said smiling like a Cheshire cat. "It's all mine."

Seeing that her attorney only received $125 from her share of the divorce settlement, Esteban worked out a deal with her attorney. He would pay all of her legal fees in exchange for all her personal belongings, gifted items and car. So technically, Esteban owned her stuff.

Her credit cards, cell phone and other joints accounts were cancelled. The debt was separated and she now had to pay her own credit card bills.

He didn't stop there. He informed her that he was the new owner of the vacation home in Punta Cana. He filed an injunction in court the day after Darlene got back from assessing the properties. He proved it was an endangerment to sell the property "as-is" due to all of the damages and negligence on her behalf. Esteban provided copies of the assessment reports from the engineers as proof. He also provided several estimates of how much it would cost to correct those mistakes, which there were plenty of. He was willing to pay for it upfront in order to sell the house since they had a signed contract on it already. However, he wanted to be reimbursed out of her share of the profits. The court agreed and gave him ownership of her percentage since the cost of the repairs totaled more than her share was worth. He showed her that document as well.

Then, he added that there really was no buyer. He just needed a signed contract demonstrating that she would sell even at the risk of others. But the kicker was, he'd paid the engineers to write those false reports. He needed them as evidence for the court. And the engineer she hired was the brother to his. So, they told the same story. But, the house was really worth $2.4 million.

She started cursing him out, but Esteban didn't care. He just kept on adding insult to injury.

When she blabbed about Carlos in front of everyone, it created witnesses. So, he filed another injunction to obtain their prestigious hotel and two restaurants since it had all been acquired with his money anyway. It now belonged to Esteban. Along with the collection of cars, money from their bank accounts and the home in Cabarete since neither one could afford it. Police seized everything once she got on the plane to come back.

"You Mother Fucker! I HATE YOU!" she yelled.

Esteban laughed as he kept cutting into her.

He admitted he's known about her and Carlos for a while. She gave him reason to have them investigated. But he wasn't sure she knew everything about her beloved Carlos. For instance, he had been married for ten years and has three kids. And he had set them up pretty well with Maritza's money.

Over the course of time, he acquired nine income-generating properties throughout D.R. and had a secret bank account with five million dollars in it from the income of those properties. Carlos also purchased his family a gigantic home in Santo Domingo, a yacht and a hair salon for his wife. But, the big business was his income generating property and hotel on the Cayman Islands. Carlos had franchised his hotel and branched out.

"You're lying! You're a liar!" she said screaming and yelling.

Apparently, Maritza had no clue. So, he politely handed her an envelope with pictures showing it all. He even showed her copies of the ownership records with his name on everything. It was all seized as well.

But Esteban wasn't quite done. He revealed that he'd purposely opened a branch office of his accounting firm in the Dominican Republic. His General Manager sought them out and persuaded them to do business with him. That's how he knew about all of their businesses, the three off-shore accounts mentioned in court and the money coming in from the rental house in Punta Cana. All of their money was handled by his firm.

He saw that Carlos was a smart man when it came to business. So, Esteban sat back this whole time and watched Carlos make him richer.

"And by the way, you really didn't make bad investments. I just made it look like you did. I actually made $179,200 on you," said Esteban laughing.

He put the icing on the cake. He waved his fingers for Darlene and Lola to come out. He started with Darlene.

He put his arm around her and kissed her. It felt so good telling Maritza that Darlene was his new woman. He traded Maritza's car in and bought Darlene a new white Maserati Gran Turisomo. He gave her all of the jewelry in the bank safe. But the best part was telling her he'd purchased the mansion on East 70th Street for them to live in. Maritza got really angry because she'd always wanted him to buy it for her, but he never would. Then, he put his other arm around Lola hugging her tight. He shared that he found his missing child with Amelia. It was Lola. And she was the one who bought the penthouse for twenty dollars. He just had it remodeled as a gift to his daughter and two sons who now called it home. He spent over $1 million on upgrades.

"You Son of a Bitch!!!" screamed Maritza over and over.

"Oh…And your boyfriend had to give up his brownstone in Brooklyn. Wouldn't you know it…He couldn't afford it without you," said Esteban laughing.

She just lost it. She lunged at him, but was on the floor before she realized it. The officers intervened pushing her down to the ground. Once she was in handcuffs, she was pulled up to her feet. Esteban had one last thing to tell her.

He got really close to her and whispered in her ear, "I'm richer than you can ever imagine" and told her his worth.

She went to kick him, but Lola blocked it. He stepped back and said, "You've hurt, used and lived off me and our kids for the last time. You've made our lives a living hell and now I hope yours becomes one. So as EJ would say…Step off BITCH!" he said walking away with his two favorite girls.

But Lola turned around and did it. "And this is for my mother," she said spitting in her face.

Maritza went crazy as she was carted off to jail.

Chapter 45
<u>Family Meeting</u>

That same evening, Esteban called a family meeting. Lola, Mauricio and EJ hosted it in their new penthouse. Darlene and Amanda were there as well. And he invited his two sisters and their husbands over.

Esteban updated his sisters on everything that happened in court. They were happy he was finally divorced.

Next, he told them about Lola being his biological daughter and explained that entire story.

But the hardest thing was telling them about Mauricio. They were shocked to hear what Maritza had done, but assured their nephew nothing would change. They loved him and adored him. He had their support and could count on them for anything. Mauricio was grateful and appreciated it.

Once his sisters left, Esteban talked to the kids about what he'd acquired in the divorce settlement.

He gave the mansion in Cabarete to Mauricio and Lola. EJ kept the vacation home in Punta Cana. He gave the Brownstone in Brooklyn to Amanda. And they decided what to do with the money in the offshore accounts.

After, Esteban talked about remodeling the hotel and the two restaurants in D.R. He planned to make them a little more upscale than what they already were. But EJ had no clue what he was talking about. They forgot he wasn't there that morning Maritza ranted and revealed everything. So, they told him the whole story.

The last order of business was telling them about Carlos and all he had acquired behind Maritza's back. They were surprised, but didn't blame him. Maritza was stupid and careless.

Esteban kept the hotel and the mega mansion on the Cayman Islands. He traded in the yacht and got Mauricio the one he wanted, a Marquis 720 tri-deck. It was a little bit bigger than Lola's Marquis 500SB, but they now owned two yachts. Esteban kept the five million dollars. And he wasn't sure what to do with the wife's salon. However, they each had to choose two properties out of the ten that Carlos owned.

Mauricio chose the 12-bedroom luxury oceanfront estate in La Romana and the 10-bedroom beachfront mansion in Cabrera.

Lola got the 11-bedroom oceanfront palace in Playa Grande and a 5-bedroom waterfront villa in Rio San Juan.

EJ chose a 4-bedroom exclusive mountain hacienda in Sosua and a 6-bedroom private hilltop estate in Puerto Plata.

Amanda picked a 6-bedroom estate on a golf course in Punta Cana and a 4-level, 6-bedroom villa in Las Terrenas.

Esteban kept the 8-bedroom luxury villa in Cabrera and Carlos' 13-bedroom family home in Santo Domingo.

Esteban just had a few surprises left.

"Amanda, how would you feel about me marrying your mother?" asked Esteban. "And please be honest."

"And the same for you," said Darlene referring to his three kids.

All of them were okay with their parents getting married. Esteban treated Darlene well, which was Amanda's concern. And Darlene wasn't out for his money, which was his kids' concern.

So, Esteban took a ring box out of his pocket. It was an original Harry Winston engagement ring. The 22-carat, asscher-cut diamond had a single band of micro pavé diamonds. Everyone yelled, screamed and congratulated them. Hugs and kisses were passed around.

Next, Esteban handed Amanda a Mercedes Benz key. He told her to go to his dealership and pick out anyone she wanted. She screamed, yelled and hugged Esteban tight. Darlene thanked him, too.

The last thing was a gift for Lola. He handed Lola a box. Inside were a key and a restaurant flyer. David helped Esteban franchise her restaurant into the New York market. She now owned an Esperanza's in New York.

"Thanks, Dad," she said hugging him.

"You're welcome, Míja," he said tearing. Esteban never got tired of hearing her call him that.

Chapter 46
Spain

Esteban was turning the big 5-0. He wanted to celebrate his birthday with his family in Spain. He had more shocking secrets to reveal.

The guest list included Carmela and Camelia with their entire families, Darlene, Amanda, his kids, Ana and David, Crystale and Wyatt, Blair and Ivan and Robert and Janelle with their daughter.

They flew into Barcelona the Friday before his big day. The ride towards the Mediterranean coast was about forty minutes.

They pulled up to Esteban's castle that sat on a hill with a panoramic view of the countryside and the Mediterranean Sea. Its stone exterior gave it that castle look. The interior was three stories with fifteen bedrooms, seventeen bathrooms, large open spaces, high ceilings, classic and rustic elements, an Olympic size pool, an acre of gardens, terraces and fruit trees, a golf course and marina.

They relaxed Friday evening. They got in kind of late and wanted to be refreshed for the big day.

On Saturday, they spent most of his birthday on his yacht. It was bright and sunny, but a bit chilly. The temperature had only gotten up to the lower 60's.

Later that evening, Esteban planned a dinner party. He invited a few of his close friends from there and invited a special guest.

Lola and Mauricio were the first to come down after changing for dinner.

"Oh my God! You look just like her," said a man approaching Lola. "You're so beautiful. A spitting image of her."

Lola smiled and said, "Thank you, but who are you talking about?"

"Your grandmother."

"You knew my grandmother?"

"Yes."

Esteban introduced him as Marcos Alonso.

As the others trickled down, they adjourned to the dining room. It was so beautifully decorated and there was enough food to feed an army.

Esteban introduced his family to his additional guests. Then, he asked if Marcos Alonso could tell them a story as they sat and ate dinner. They didn't mind.

A long time ago when he was young, Marcos Alonso and his father often traveled. His father wanted him to learn the family business being the only son and his heir.

Cuba was one of the countries they often visited for business. While there, his family always stayed in the best suite at Copa Havana Hotel in Havana. It was the most prestigious hotel at the time. Not to mention, they had the best entertainment.

Every night, there were live shows with lights, music and dancing. Plenty of showgirls hit the stage with their over-the-top costumes and choreographed performances that entertained the crowd.

One night, Marcos Alonso sat in the audience enjoying the show. Halfway through, a beautiful young lady came on stage and performed a solo. He was mesmerized by her. He watched her every move in amazement. He had to have her.

During that time, showgirls were off limits to the guests. Men had the cabaret situated on the other side of the hotel to fulfill any of their sexual pleasures.

And there were rules. Women from the cabaret were never allowed to go up to a man's hotel room. And the showgirls were never allowed to serve in the cabaret. The showgirls were considered top of the line and untouchable. If these rules were broken, they'd suffer major consequences.

But Marcos Alonso didn't care. He went after what he wanted by paying big bucks for this young lady to put on a private show later that night. And she was obligated because it made the hotel more money. But he was not to get involved with her because they came from different social classes. She was poor. He wasn't.

He waited for her after work. He asked her to meet him at a secret location. He even offered her money. But she declined for fear of what could happen to her.

The next night, he caught her before she entered the hotel for work. He asked the same question and again she declined.

So later that night, he wore a mask and snatched her up as she was riding her bike home. He took her to a secret location nearby. When he took off the mask, Marcos Alonso remembered how apologetic he was for scaring her. But figured that was the only way she would spend time with him and not get in trouble. He was right.

She eventually loosened up and became very acquainted with him. They secretly met every night that week.

Marcos Alonso remembered going back to Cuba every three days for a month after they met. He knew he was treading on thin ice by being around this young woman, but again he didn't care. They had fallen for each other.

One night, he couldn't take being without her anymore. So, he snuck over to her house. When she saw him, she just about died. He wasn't supposed to be there. It could get her family in trouble, possibly killed, if anyone found out. He handed her some money and asked her to meet him at a new location. She agreed and rushed him off.

She lost her virginity to him that night. They made passionate love over and over again. And they continued seeing each other for another month.

Then all hell broke loose. His father caught wind of his frequent visits to Cuba and his relationship with the young woman. He disapproved and forbade Marcos Alonso to see her anymore. So on his final trip, Marcos Alonso confessed who he really was.

But that wasn't all. He was getting married in two months to a woman he barely knew. It was an arranged marriage between families. They were in the same social class and it was good for business. And even though he didn't want to, he didn't have a choice.

She was devastated and broken hearted. But the worse part was yet to come.

A woman Marcos Alonso used to sleep with at the cabaret got jealous of their relationship. So, she told on this young woman. She was banned from working at the hotel. Also, her grandmother and brother were kidnapped.

When Marcos Alonso heard what happened, he knew he had to help her. So, he snuck back into Cuba without his parents' knowledge. He went to her house and kidnapped her. Once she realized who it was, she just hugged and kissed him. They made love right there.

After, he handed her a black duffle bag full of jewels and cash. There were also visas, passports and a few phone numbers of people in different countries, if she needed help. She was to guard it with her life.

He explained that she couldn't go back home. That was the deal he made to ensure her family's safety. So, she was on her own and had to take care of herself.

Then, he slipped an engagement ring on her finger symbolizing his love. Since he couldn't marry her, it was to remember him by. They made love again for the last time.

"Did you ever see this young woman again?" blurted Lola in the middle of the story.

"No. I couldn't. And it was for her safety," said Marcos Alonso.

Dinner was over. Esteban's friends left while Ana, David, his kids, their friends and Darlene went to the terrace where Marcos Alonso finished the story.

Marcos Alonso arranged for her to leave the country that very same night. He told her where to go and begged her not to miss her ride. They hugged very tight and declared one another as their true love. That was the last time he saw her.

Her transportation was a boat ride to Spain. Once there,

she could travel to any country she wanted to go to with her visas and passports. But she was never to exchange any of the jewels in the bag while in Spain.

She decided to get a hotel room and some food for the night. She was tired and needed to think. She also needed a place to empty the bag to check out its contents. There were diamonds, emeralds, rubies, pearls, lots of cash and legal citizenship in three different countries. She understood why he said what he did.

A few days later, she found out she was pregnant. She decided to stay in Spain to find him. She tried one of those numbers he gave her and desperately looked for him. But Marcos Alonso was not to be reached.

She eventually started working and moved into her own place. She met a man who gave her and her child a last name. They got married and moved to the United States two years later.

"Wow! What a story," said Lola. "But how did you know she had a child if you never spoke to her again?"

"The question you asked was if I saw her again and my reply was that I had not. And that's the truth. But I did speak to her a few times on the telephone. She told me everything," said Marcos Alonso.

"So, do you know who your son is?" she asked happy for him.

"Yes."

Then, Esteban formally introduced him.

"This is Marcos Alonso Santa Cruz del Los Torres better known as His Majesty, King Marcos Alonso of Spain," said Esteban.

Mouths dropped open.

"You should probably explain, Esteban," said Marcos Alonso chuckling at their facial expressions.

King Marcos Alonso was Esteban's biological father. The woman in the story was his mother, Patricia. She fell in love with him when he was His Royal Highness, Prince Marcos Alonso of Leon. And running the country of Spain was the family business. Forming an alliance with the Cuban government was part of that business. That was the reason for the frequent visits.

And even though he loved Patricia, he had to marry Her Royal Highness, Princess Claudia of Zamora.

Patricia met Guillermo Hernandez while in Spain. He accepted Esteban as his son and later they had twin daughters, Camelia and Carmela.

But Marcos Alonso had always kept tabs on them.

"So that's where all the jewelry came from?" asked Mauricio.

"Yes. I gave it to her long ago," said Marcos Alonso. "And Lola's ring is the very same one I put on your grandmother's finger."

Then, Lola jumped up imitating Queen Elizabeth's wave realizing her bloodline. "I'm really a princess. Like a real princess."

Everyone just laughed at her.

"It's Her Royal Highness from now on, People," said Lola still waving .

"Not quite, Míja," said Esteban still laughing.

Marcos Alonso explained how illegitimate children could never have rights to the throne and aren't recognized as royalty. So even as his firstborn, Esteban would never be known as a king or royalty because of it. He was fine with it. Esteban enjoyed their relationship the way it currently was. And he wouldn't trade Guillermo and what he taught him for the world.

Chapter 47
Lola's Princess Wedding

The wedding of the century had finally arrived. Lola and Mauricio were getting married. And it was an occasion fit for a princess.

Lola's way of doing things was always over the top and extravagant. That meant a big production with lots of color, carats and bling. So, her wedding wouldn't be any different.

Lola's magic day was taking place at the Waldorf Astoria Hotel and Resort in Boca Raton. This prestigious venue was known for its signature weddings and luxurious accommodations.

Lola and most of her out-of-town guests stayed in the Tower. She had the two-story Presidential Suite on the 26th floor.

This beautiful penthouse suite had three bedrooms, a marble master bath with jetted tub, full kitchen, media room and a grand piano. She also had the best view of the Intracoastal Waterway and Atlantic Ocean.

The hotel accommodated Lola's request for early morning spa services for her entire wedding party. She wanted everyone to look and feel refreshed for the event.

She created her own spa package, including full body massages, body wraps, waxings, facials, manicures and pedicures.

A pre-ceremony cocktail hour began promptly at 4:00 p.m. for Lola's on-time guests. It took place on the terrace at the Yacht Club.

Uniquely shaped white modular sofas with mirrored cocktail tables filled the space. White sheer paneling draped across the sky creating canopies of shade. Gorgeous white floral arrangements of Phalaenopsis orchids, ostrich plume feathers and draping crystals sat in sparkly covered vases and were on display. Four to seven foot tall albino, floral sculpted peacocks fashioned the entrance and white banisters. The Intracoastal made for a beautiful background. And her guests enjoyed music, glasses of champagne and a limited variety of appetizers.

One of the biggest reasons Lola chose the Waldorf was the Cathedral Room. The hotel designed, built and staged a building to look like a cathedral. This made it possible for guests to have their wedding in a church-like setting without any religious hassles.

The exterior looked like a Roman Cathedral with its Neo-Gothic architecture, cathedral facade, towering spires, flying buttresses and figurines.

The inside was just as amazing. The nave had a long center aisle, domed ceilings, soft lighting and giant columns separating the side aisles. The Romanesque architectural detailing included angelic murals, round arches, stain glass windows, mosaic artwork and marble flooring. The altar had an extravagant brass baldacchino. And there was seating for 500.

Lola reserved limousines for the bridal party and a white 1956 vintage Bentley for herself. Even though the ceremony was on the hotel's premises, she wanted photos and video of their arrival.

Lola's other favorite color was red. The more the better.

Large red floral trees were stationed over guests seating. An abundance of red fabric draped the entire room, including columns, pillars and the baldacchino. Elaborate red floral arrangements on different sized pedestals, glass vases filled with ice rocks and candles created the wide center aisle. Tons of red rose petals were laid as an aisle runner. Giant chandeliers, hanging candles and tons of draping crystals made the room sparkle.

All of the men in the wedding party wore custom made white Ermenegildo Zegna tuxedos with 5-button jackets and white Prada shoes. The groomsmen wore their tuxedos with a red vest, tie, handkerchief and boutonniere. EJ wore the same thing, but in gold.

They all wore gold Rolex diamond watches and 2-carat gold and diamond bracelets that Mauricio gifted them.

Mauricio wore his all white tuxedo with a white boutonniere. His jewelry was custom-made by Graff.

He splurged on a sparkling 20-carat diamond watch, a 14-carat diamond bracelet and 3-carat diamond square studs for each ear.

The bridesmaids wore red ball gowns. Their red, satin bodices had sweetheart necklines with floral appliqués and intricate Swarovski crystal detailing. The satin and chiffon ruffled skirts layered into a chapel train with a floral gathered design on the sides.

They wore red Stuart Weitzman with diamond-encrusted heels, gold and ruby double headbands with two red flowers on the side and gold and ruby Indian-styled jewelry sets that Lola gifted them. And their bouquets were made of red roses with gold and bling embellishments.

A very pregnant Crystale wore a gold, satin halter dress with a fully beaded top and chiffon layered over the satin. Her gold Stuart Weitzman pumps had a low heel. Her hair was worn up with a wide, gold flowered headband. Lola gifted her with a gold Indian-styled jewelry set. And her bouquet was filled with gold-dusted white roses and sparkly embellishments.

The ceremony began promptly at 5:00 p.m. The processional began with the officiant walking down the aisle towards the altar and four flower girls releasing red rose petals after him. Ana and Mauricio followed behind. Darlene and EJ entered next. Fifteen groomsmen and bridesmaids proceeded after them, with Crystale tailing at the end. The ring bearer was the last to enter before the bride.

When Celine Dion's *'Love doesn't ask why'* came on, everyone stood to there feet. Six more flower girls walked the aisle, releasing more red rose petals.

Then, the doors opened. Lola stood there with David and Esteban on each arm. Mauricio's eyes watered when he saw her.

Lola wore an original princess ball gown designed by Yumi Katsura for her ceremony. It was big and extreme. The white, strapless gown had a sheer corset with a sweetheart neckline and heavy crystal and pearl detailing. The fully bustled skirt had voluminous bubble hems cascading down into a cathedral train. There was a piece of jeweled tulle with crystal floral appliqués in the front. And circular ruffled patterns created floral designs throughout the skirt of the dress.

Her diamond-encrusted shoes were by Christian Louboutin. Her hair was worn in a high curled bun with a princess tiara. And Lola's Indian-styled jewelry was custom made by Graff as well.

Her double collared necklace totaled 125-carats. The top collar had round, pear and emerald cut diamonds with hanging strands of diamonds and pearls in platinum. The elongated collar had the same round, pear and emerald cut diamonds with longer strands of diamonds and pearls. The 20-carat chandelier earrings had the same craftsmanship as the necklace. And she wore over 30 carats in different diamond and pearl bracelets.

Her cascading bouquet was a masterpiece. The combination of white flowers included Cymbidium orchids, roses, peony, freesia, tulips and sweet peas. Diamond jeweled flowers with crystal and pearl pins accessorized her bouquet. The stems were wrapped in satin with rhinestone rings, strands of draping crystals and tiny pictures of her and Mauricio in diamond frames.

The ceremony took about forty minutes with prayers, scripture readings and the exchanging of their own vows and wedding bands. They exchanged similar 5-carat, platinum round and baguette diamond Eternity bands

Lola's 350 guests were escorted to the hotel's luxurious styled garden for the cocktail hour. White sheer panels in crisscross patterns stretched across the entire area. The white and gold, mosaic tiled fountain drizzled in diamond strands. Romantic lighting with multitudes of white candles created an intimate setting. Sculptured trees and landscaping added drama to the space. White designer fabrics dressed the circular and squared contemporary sofas, chairs and tables. White rose petals covered the entire lawn. Two to three foot tall floral swan sculptures and floating candles filled the pool. And guests mingled as they enjoyed the open bar and an array of appetizers.

The Venetian Palace Ballroom embodied regal elegance with contemporary charm. This grand room had coffered ceilings, arched glass wooden doors and thick marble Roman columns that emanated old world class. Large windows with posh window treatments overlooked the ocean. And guests sat underneath a sea of large crystal chandeliers that hung from the ceiling.

Lola added her red to this already beautiful room. Long pieces of red sheer panels formed elongated, dome-shaped designs that hung from the ceiling throughout the room. Five foot tall gold candelabras with huge, red intricate floral arrangements and draping crystals sat as centerpieces. The tables were dressed in red satin while the gold chiavari chairs had giant red satin rose chair caps. Gold charger plates with fan-shaped edging, red napkins with gold floral napkin rings and gold silverware beautified the tables. Gold tree branches with red flowers and crystal strands filled the room. And red uplighting illuminated the space.

Her cake had its own area. This colossal display consisted of a 4-tiered, squared center cake with a red and gold damask pattern. It sat one foot off the table with a mini water fountain underneath. Four red, 2-tiered, round cakes sat on each corner connected by lighted crystal staircases and bridges. They sat six inches off the table creating height for the bed of red rose petals that covered the entire table.

The entire wedding party changed. The groomsmen wore white linen suits with long sleeve Guayabera tops. The bridesmaids slipped into red, fitted halter dresses with rhinestone embellishments and front splits. Mauricio changed into a white Prada suit and Lola's dress was scandalous.

Zuhair Murad designed her second dress. It was red, sleeveless and had a high-collared neckline. The bodice had an elaborate floral pattern with beaded embroidery on sheer silk. The skirt was feathered with a waist-high split on the side.

Lola and Mauricio heard whistles and screams as they entered the ballroom as newlyweds. They went straight to the smoked filled dance floor to dance to N Sync's Spanish version of *'This I promise you'*.

Then, Marc Anthony's *'Nadie Como Ella'* came on. Lights flashed as they danced salsa. Their bridesmaids and groomsmen joined in for a choreographed routine. It ended with confetti shooting out all over the room.

Lola changed for the third and final time. Her custom made dress by Vera Wang was white, sparkly and fitted. It was a fully beaded and pearled halter dress with a low back and plunging V neckline. It had a split up the side and a small train.

During dinner, EJ and Crystale stood up to make their best man and matron of honor speeches. Blair, Wyatt, Robert, Ana, David and Esteban also said a few words.

After, Lola and Mauricio's friends had an announcement.

"Good evening everyone. Can I have your attention?" said Blair tapping the microphone.

"We're here because we have a very special surprise for our friends," said Wyatt.

A waiter took the newlyweds an envelope.

"Mr. and Mrs. Hernandez...We'd like to present you with a ten-day Arabian honeymoon," said Ivan passing the microphone.

"First, you'll spend three days at the Banyan Tree Resort on the private island of Maldives. You'll enjoy an ocean villa while in a sanctuary of relaxation," said Crystale.

"Then, you'll jet off to the Burj Al Arab Hotel in Dubai for seven days. You'll enjoy seven-star luxury amenities and great shopping," said Wyatt.

"This all-expense paid trip is filled with many romantic surprises for you to enjoy. And PLEASE...Come back pregnant," said Blair being funny.

Everyone laughed and cheered as the newlyweds went over to hug their friends.

As the party was happening, Mauricio pulled his wife close to him.

"I love you, Baby Girl," he said.

"I love you, too, Baby," she said.

"You're stuck with me now. You know this is forever."

"That's how long I want to love you, Baby."

Book Club Questions

1. What did you like about the book?

2. Did you feel that the book fulfilled your expectations? Were you disappointed?

3. Did you enjoy the book? Why? Why not?

4. What about the plot? Did it pull you in; or did you feel forced to read it?

5. What passage from the book stood out the most?

6. Are there situations and/or characters that you can identify with? Why not?

7. Which character do you like the most and why? The least and why?

8. Did you learn something you didn't know?

9. Name your favorite thing about the book. Name your least favorite.

10.	Did the book end the way you expected?

11.	At what point did you decide if you liked the book? What helped you?

12.	If you could change one thing about the book, what would it be?

13.	What major emotion did the story evoke in you as a reader?

14.	Have you had a life changing revelation from reading this text?

15.	Would you recommend this book to other readers?

Bella Dama was born in New York, but raised in California. She eventually moved to Miami, Florida with her two small children. She lived there until recently, she now resides in North Carolina.

This is the author's first novel. She has worked in Human Resources for over 20 years and is now venturing out on a new path.

You may write Bella Dama at PO Box 480677, Charlotte, NC 28269, or visit her website at www.labelladama.net.

From a Proverbs 31 Woman